Cavewoman

J. N. FOXE

CAVEWOMAN

Contents

Chapter 1

Prologue

"Charlotte!"

I sit up suddenly with a paper stuck to my cheek from my drool. Classic. I remove said paper and look up from my desk at my boss who is looking down at me, unhappy.

"Yes, Mr. Davis?" I croak and clear my throat. God, how long was I out?

"I've been calling your phone and standing here for more time than I can spare. If you weren't my top broker you'd be packing your things!" He sighs and clears his throat. I inwardly roll my eyes as he rubs his temples and recites whatever mumbo jumbo his latest yogi taught him. With his temper reigned in he turns on me again.

"Charlotte, we are on a deadline and I need you at your best. I know I've put a lot on you, but I'm counting on you to land the Brinkmann account or else both of our heads will be on the chopping block next week."

My face always gives away my feelings and it must have done just so during his speech.

"I guess you might feel overworked and under-appreciated, but those feelings don't bring home the bacon. Just stuff that stress and anxiety deep, deep down." He presses down imaginary stress into a box with his hands. "You can relax and sleep after we close the account and get that commission."

I nod my agreement, and he stomps back to his corner office, most likely to call his mistress for dinner plans. I grab my purse and walk toward the bathroom to collect myself when I feel a sharp stabbing pain in my chest. It keeps getting worse as I go in and lock the door. I rub my chest to no avail. Now it feels like there's a vise squeezing my rib cage. God, I'm dying. Obituary will read, "Dead from heart attack at 35." I lie down on the tile floor and place my cheek against the cool tile. I'm crying because I want to die and end all of the stress, but I'm also crying because I don't want to die. I just want a simpler life. I want to be happy. But I have to stay in this job because of my lease on the condo and my car loan and the bills. I don't want to die because I don't want Kevin to find me like this. As much as I want to simply stop breathing, I don't want to hurt him, so I give myself five minutes to cry on the floor of the bathroom. I take a Xanax from my purse and roll onto my back, focusing on my breathing and counting the ceiling tiles until I feel the benzos kick in. That always calms me.

Once I can breathe normally and the anxiety has receded, I take a paper towel, wet it and pat my forehead and neck. It feels cool and grounds me. I look hard into the mirror.

"It wasn't supposed to be like this," I say to the woman in the mirror.

Smoothing back my hair and straightening my jacket and skirt, I take a deep breath and exit the bathroom making a mental battle plan about how I'm going to persuade the Brinkmanns to allow us to manage their extensive financial portfolio and assets. The commission from this one alone would pay for Kevin and I to go on our dream vacation for our ten year anniversary.

I shut down my laptop and gather my things to go home. The last to leave the office, as usual, I turn off the lights and lock the door behind me. It's ten p.m., and by the time I drive home, Kevin will already be in bed. I'll be out the door in the morning before he wakes, too. Our marriage can't withstand much more of this; I wouldn't blame him if he left me, but I don't know where I would go. I could be cruel and keep the condo, but I wouldn't do that to him. My father is in D.C. working at the Pentagon, and my mother lives in a tiny one-bedroom loft close to her office in the city. Even if they had space, I would avoid living with them at all costs; a hotel would be better.

Being so busy has stripped all my friendships down to casual Facebook friends, so I have no one to turn to. I send up a silent prayer for Kevin to hold on a little longer. I know I need to change, but this success and money is addictive; it's my crack, and I can't live without it. There's no person that wakes up one morning and thinks, "I want to be an addict." Addiction is slow and seductive. The worst are the legal ones. At the rate I'm abusing these drugs, though, I'm not going to live to see forty. I pray, "God, if there's any way possible, help me change. I'm desperate— I'll do anything."

Chapter 2

Day 0

"*Sometimes what we think we want is not what we need.*"
-Harley King

Nothing gets better than this. The sun, the cool crisp air, the increased heart rate from the climb up the mountain were exactly what we needed. All the hard work the last year that paid for this trip; these moments have made it worth it. Mostly. I stop and put my hands on my hips, arching my back and feeling the warm sun on my cheeks. I wish I could bottle up this air, this sun, this moment and take it back with me. Or better yet, not go back.

"Hey Kev? Can we rest a minute?" I'm panting.

Kevin looks back and gives me his million megawatt smile that stops my heart every time. "Sure babe." He drops his pack by his feet, grabbing his water canteen, and sits down cross-legged. He's in his element, and it's satisfying to watch his sure movements and agility. "You want a granola bar?"

"I'm good for now. Just need a break." I sit down too and stretch my legs out in front of me. My calves and glutes are cramped and spasming— I'm nearing muscle fatigue. We both just breathe for a while and take in the view. Nothing but blue sky and snow-capped mountains. "I wish I could freeze this moment and live here forever."

Kevin grabs my hand and kisses the back tenderly. "You can't appreciate the beauty of the mountaintop view without drudging through the valley first."

I roll my eyes at him and yank back my hand. "If I wanted a sermon I'd call my pastor. God needs to fix His math because I've had way more valleys than mountains." I do a few stretches to work out my cramps then lie back in the grass and watch fluffy white clouds lazily float by. "I just didn't think being an adult would be this hard. When I was young I daydreamed about my Prince Charming, getting married in a beautiful dress, living in a castle and having lots of babies. Nowhere in there was a wish for a stressful career and stacks of bills. I need a change, but I can't seem to find the exit on the freeway."

There's an awkward silence, so long that I roll my head over to look at him and make sure he hasn't fallen asleep. He looks at me innocently and raises his hands, "Oh, I didn't know your monologue was over. Am I allowed to talk now?"

I cover my face with my hands and make a mock growl of frustration even though I'm silently laughing. Kev has kept me laughing since I met him. He even put it in his wedding vows to make me laugh everyday.

"You already know what I'm going to say. Leave your job and find something that fulfills you and brings you joy. Or even don't work. Take some time and stay at home and recenter. This is your first vacation in years and that's not healthy, even if your commission did have six zeros. How much money would you give in the moment of a panic attack if it could take your anxiety away?"

Big sigh. He's right, again. "I just need time. It's scary making that kind of a change, but I will promise to think about it." There's a grunt that I know means he doesn't believe me. I stand up and brush the dirt off my legs and butt. "I'm going to go use the ladies room behind that bush over there, Kev," I call out behind me as I head toward the tall shrub. I shouldn't be embarrassed to go to the bathroom in front of him after ten years of marriage, but I just can't.

The terrain this high up the mountain is a mixture of loose rocks and boulders that have rolled down the mountain, wild grasses, scraggly bushes and pine trees. I walk behind the bushes and climb up on a large rock. Jumping off big rocks always gave me a high, and it got me into trouble many times. Feeling youthful and energetic, I climb up and jump off with a squeal.

Kevin

I'm leaning against a warm rock, waiting on Charlotte to come back from the bathroom. I could easily doze off, but it would be a shame to waste even a second of this once-in-a-lifetime vacation. The sky is so blue it almost looks fake. Just some stringy white clouds cling to the tips of mountains like cotton candy. If I took a picture of this now and showed it to people back home they would probably think it was AI generated. Why don't we do this more often? Connect, communicate, have adventures. It's not a lack of love for each other because when we're together we act like lovebirds, but life has a way of choking the fun out. This trip has been a peaceful moment to just exhale and be present.

This tranquil moment now feels a little too long. I glance at my watch. I'm not sure what time she went to the bathroom, but it's been several minutes. I call out, "Char! Everything coming out ok?" This would normally elicit a snarky response or at least a "Shut up, Kevin." The silence makes me worried that she's up to something ornery. Even though she wanted privacy, I turn so that I can check on her. I can see the bush she said she was going to pee behind. A large rock behind it, maybe four feet high, is barely visible through the branches. Oh no. Charlotte was a bit of a daredevil in her younger years; I would bet money that she was back there doing her old gymnastics routine and jumping off to "stick the landing." I hear a squeal and see her arms and ponytail fly up in the air. Then everything is quiet.

I count ten Mississippi's and then stand up and brush my pants off. I'll just sneak around the bush the other way and give her a little scare. I'm walking on my tiptoes on the other side of the large shrub I saw her go behind, but she's not there. I look around. Hmmmm. I expand out to see if she's hiding, waiting to jump scare me, but still nothing. I call out, "Char! Charlotte! Where are you?" No response. This little joke isn't funny any-more. "This isn't the place to be joking around, Char! You could get hurt!"

A little bubble of panic is starting to build up in my chest. I was a Boy Scout, and I remember how we learned to track game. This time the tracks I'm looking for are size seven hiking boots. I return the way I came and follow her tracks to the rock. The tracks stop at the rock. Just past the rock are some loose rocks and dirt that look recently disturbed but no tracks. No blood. Nothing to the left or right. Something about this spot is bothering me. No grass or weeds. My training tells me this is not manmade. It doesn't have a regular shape like it would if it had been dug up or filled in with a shovel. The ground looks like something sank in it, then these rocks and dirt rolled in and filled the hole. I don't have any equipment with me so I examine the area manually. It is about four feet across at the widest point. I touch the ground, feeling for density and consistency. It's firm but is not packed tight on the surface. I brush the loose top layer of rocks off with my hand and feel something hard. I grab it and dust it off. It's Charlotte's Apple Watch.

There are no tracks past this spot. The ground appears recently disturbed. I have to calm my fears and think critically. For heaven's sake, I have a master's in geology and a doctorate in archaeology; surely I can solve this problem. Logically speaking there is only one conclusion to draw. She came over here, her tracks stopped, and she dropped a personal item. She didn't go past this spot, and she can't go up ,so she must've gone down. My understanding of rock formations and how the ground is constantly shifting and moving, sometimes in completely unpredictable ways, leads me to believe that it is entirely possible that she could have fallen in a sinkhole or through a crack. She could be just feet below the surface or even possibly hundreds of feet.

I must investigate this spot and determine, if at all possible, what type of rock composition we are dealing with. I brush my hands over the disturbed rocks, swiping away the loose dirt and grass. What I see next horrifies me. There is no crack or hole. It is a solid piece of granite that has shifted to block the entrance of whatever opening she possibly fell into. I have nothing with me to get through it or even dig around it. I sit back on my heels and stare at it in complete disbelief. I've been on digs around the world and felt confident in excavating into caves, temples and ancient remains buried deep in desserts and under dense jungles. This is impenetrable and impossible given my current tools and supplies and lack of manpower. My brain is telling me the best thing I can do is hike down the mountain to get help, but I don't want to leave. I'm worried that she could emerge somewhere else on the mountain after I've left and not be able to find her way back. She didn't have her pack: no water or food. I can't dwell on the facts I know about how long a person can go without those. I have to be positive. I have to hope. I have to get help.

Before it gets dark, I search the area around the rock in widening circles until I'm convinced she did not go past this rock, at least not above ground. With a frustrated groan I go back to get our packs and gear. I hold back a cry when I pick up her girly pink Columbia backpack with a floral print. When she picked it out I rolled my eyes.

She said, "What? It's not like you have to carry it."

Wow, she was wrong. Using her backpack as a pillow and her coat as a blanket, I curl up and give myself over to the tears that I have held back all day. My eyes close, but I don't sleep. There's a horror film playing on the backs of my eyelids that would make Steven King's books look like bedtime stories.

Chapter 3

Day 1

Into nothing. The darkness is suffocating; the silence deafening. I have that moment you get when you wake up in the morning and you are sensing everything around you before you open your eyes: birds chirping, the smell of coffee, a full bladder, sore neck. In this case I am markedly aware of the lack of light. I haven't opened my eyes, but I know that it is dark, like in my bones. Fear was sneaking up behind me like the grim reaper, wrapping its bony fingers around my neck, making me feel like I couldn't breathe. "Please, not another panic attack," I whisper.

I decide to count to three and open my eyes. One, two, three. Nope—I'm not ready yet because once I open my eyes, it's real. If I keep them shut this might be a dream, or more likely a nightmare. I am having a mental boxing match with myself and losing when I hear a drip, followed by an echo. Until then I hadn't thought about it, but not only is it dark but deathly quiet. The fingers of fear clutched my neck again, and I sit up gasping for air. Sitting up, eyes opened, I take in my surroundings; I could see my hand six inches from my face but no further. I squint my eyes looking for any pinpricks of light. Just one, directly above me. It twinkled like a distant star in a galaxy far, far away, and it seemed that far away as well. Through my pounding headache I think back to the last thing I could remember: jumping off that rock. I must have fallen down a crack or a hole, or maybe even through a wormhole. It's remotely possible that I may have to figure out where I am and also when I am. The irony is not lost on me that no one was around to hear my ironic joke. Looking around again I can safely conclude I was underground and all signs indicate a long way underground.

I decide it is ok to have a meltdown for one minute. This was a technique I learned in therapy, to allow myself to be present in my feelings, then move on. Counting to sixty, tapping each second out on my thigh, I screamed, ugly cried, and pinched the skin under my arm. When my minute is over I wipe my face with my shirt and take three cleansing breaths in and out with palms to chest. Namaste. I need to think clearly and quickly because I don't know how long I was blacked out.

Time to take inventory and assess my situation. I flexed and twisted my joints, neck and back. I am sore everywhere, but I think my posterior absorbed the biggest of the impact judging from the throbbing in my backside. I did have a large goose egg on the back of my head, and my hair was matted with blood. Several cuts on my hands from the rocks made them sticky with blood and gravel. I place my hands on either side of my hips and push up to standing, but I sit right back down after there is an immediate sharp, stabbing pain in my left ankle. I tenderly feel around my leg, ankle and foot and didn't feel any bumps or broken bones, so it must be a bad sprain. This horrible experience was going downhill rapidly.

"Breathe in, breathe out," I repeat over and over with my head between my knees. One thing at a time. What's my first step? If I'm truly as deep down as I'm afraid that I am, it could be quite a while before anyone found me or I found a way out. What do I do? The panic of disorientation and confusion is making it difficult to think rationally. What would my Eagle Scout dad tell me to do right now? He would say the most important thing for survival is water. I heard a drip earlier. I need to focus to listen again, but the panic is so loud in my head, like a Boeing 747 is taking off in my skull. I have to quiet the roar. I whisper-speak The Lord's Prayer, tapping off each repetition on my fingers to keep track of time.

"Our Father who art in Heaven," drip, "Hallowed be thy name," drip. "Your kingdom come," I pause until I hear the drip, "Your will be done," drip, "On earth as it is in Heaven," drip. "Give us this day our daily bread," drip, "and forgive us our trespasses," drip, "as we forgive those who trespass against us," drip, "and lead us not into temptation," drip, "but deliver us from the evil one," drip, "For thine is the kingdom and power and the glory forever," drip. Pause. "Amen," My exhale was punctuated by another drip. I had a friend, Drip. I needed to find her.

Walking is out of the question currently, so I scoot on my butt down the slope to what I assumed was the floor of this cave. Heading towards the sound of the drip meant that water was flowing and water travels downhill which will help me get oriented in this space. The ground is rocky and loose. The going is painful on my scraped palms and sore body. I take a break after four scoots to breathe. I'm not in the Indy 500, but I do need to keep moving. Four more scoots and I feel smooth cool rock under my hands. I listen for the drip to figure out which way to go and the sound seems to come from straight ahead. With the rock smoother now I get on all fours to crawl. I'm nervous there could be spiders and bats and snakes and other critters, so I swipe hand out in front of me before I take a crawling step forward.

Keeping the dripping in front of me, I slowly crawl forward. I can't see the light of the hole above me any-more, so I must be going deeper back in the cave. I crawl, then listen and swipe. Repeat. My eyes are be-ginning to adjust to the dark. It's still dark, but there are variations in the darkness. The ground I'm crawling on is dark gray with warm tones ,while the ceiling is pitch black and some walls are charcoal. A cool breeze brushes over my skin coming from the direction I am crawling. It smells fresh and is refreshing, so I pause to enjoy it and rest. It encourages me that I'm making progress. My mental clock tells me my break's over, so I resume crawling, when my hand that is swiping hits rock. I adjust my angle a little and feel around; it is the right wall of the cave. This must be a tunnel. I get hopeful that it will open up into a larger cavern.

I keep crawling as the tunnel continues to get narrower. Now it is so small that I have to stand carefully and squeeze through sideways, but the breeze is blowing through even faster than before and the tunnel is a shade lighter. The tunnel curves sharply to the right then I'm around the corner and pop out into the dim light of a small cavern. I stop and take in my new environment. The rock of the cavern is black and gray with silvery streaks of quartz that eerily reflect the dim light. They shoot across the rocks like distant streaks of lightning.

Four openings, including the one I am standing in, open off the cavern. I have an Indiana Jones moment where I wonder if the ground between me and the other side of the cave is booby-trapped. But before I worry about how to cross the cavern, I need to figure out which door I need to go through. The drip and fresh air have worked well so far so I try to determine which direction they are coming from.

The opening on the right is large but irregular in shape and looks unused. The one in the middle is small, about the size of a kiddie pool, and is higher off the ground. The passageway on the left looks like a small pantry door and the ground and sides appear smooth. The tunnel and cavern seemed naturally formed, but clues indicate that it may have been used by humans at some point in history. This encourages me, but the final test is if the third door has the dripping sound and fresh air current. I can faintly see the floor of the cavern, and it is relatively smooth and clear of rocks. I'm looking for any signs of wear in the rock to indicate people or animals walking there. The floor through the doorway was warmer than the others. Before I venture forward, I reach down and grab a handful of loose rocks and toss them forward across the cavern. I listen to them plunk down and settle and count to ten. There are no sounds other than my breathing and no sinking floors or arrows shooting out of the walls.

"Let's go, Short Round," I imagine Kevin saying to me.

I have to keep moving before I lose the little light I have. I can see well enough to walk forward slowly to the third door. The dripping sound is even louder than before, and the breeze caresses my face. The interior of the door is pitch black and narrow, so I put my arms straight out to my sides and shuffle forwards. Counting my steps I slowly advance through the cave, and after twenty-five steps in I can no longer see the faint light of the cavern. It's just black both ways. Fear is making this feel like a slow walk through the fun house at the fair. I've already had one meltdown today, and that's my limit. I take a deep breath in and exhale slowly then continue my march. The walls are getting wider apart, and there is a gradual lightening ahead. Five more steps and I can't touch the sides of the tunnel at all. The dripping is much louder now, so close that I can feel the spray off the drips, and it is making me realize just how thirsty I am.

The next drip lands on my shoulder and I turn to look up. A multitude of stalactites hang from the cave's ceiling, some dripping and some aren't. My eyes are adjusting and I can see a small pool of water under the dripping rocks. Looking around, the floor is cratered with puddles that all flow into a stream glowing to the right. I step into the cavern and hopscotch my way over to the stream. I'm so thirsty but nervous to drink this foreign water. But it has been filtered through the ground and is flowing and clear best I can see. I cup my hands and scoop up a small handful of water. It is cold and when I take a sip it is crisp and cool. I get another handful but it's not fast enough, so I bend down and drink out of it like a savage. After I drink my fill, and I splash water on my face and neck. This has refreshed me but also shown me how tired I am. Sitting down next to the stream I take a moment to scan my surroundings. This cavern is truly beautiful with hanging rocks looking like a medieval torture device. Kevin would have loved this, I thought, but that makes me miss him and reminds me of how alone I am. I have to keep moving because who knows how much light I have left.

Deciding to follow the stream, I crawl alongside it. The stream is getting gradually bigger as I follow it from more water feeding into it. It has grown to the size of a large creek and is flowing to the edge of the cavern. Then it flows out of sight through a small aperture. I look at it and know that I need to follow it, but I will have to lie down in the water to slide through the hole. This is a big gamble because I have no idea what is on the other side of the hole except that the water is going through it. I've survived everything so far; I pray that my luck will keep up one more time for this next crazy stunt. I lay down in the stream like I'm going down a water slide, feet first. "God, help me," I pray. Pushing off with my hands, I hold my breath and slide through.

Kevin

Sleep never came even though I was exhausted. As soon as there was enough light to see, I do another pass around the clearing, not wanting to miss a single clue. It feels wrong to leave, but there's nothing more I can do here without help.

I start down the mountain as quickly and safely as I can. The rocks are loose, and I don't want to add an injury to our list of problems. It took us two days to hike up, but even though I can hike faster without her, there's no way I can make it in just one. I can only keep walking and pray.

If anyone could hear me they would think I was certifiably insane. I'm cursing and praying and crying. "Please God, don't take her away from me. I'll do any-thing," I beg. "You said your eyes were on the righteous, and your ears are open to their prayers. I know I'm not righteous on my and I don't deserve your help. I know you can see me and hear my cries. Help us God, not because I'm good but because you are."

The trail keeps going and going—I think it got longer than the trip up. I'm trying to keep praying, to keep hoping and keep trusting, but it's hard. My mind is at war with my heart. Fear and anger are slowly eating at my insides like battery acid.

A voice is whispering, "You're not going to make it. You'll never see her again, and everyone will hate you. You will die alone."

Night falls and I curl up in a ball right in the middle of the trail, clutching Charlotte's coat and bag. The lies have taken root, and I am very afraid and mad at God.

Chapter 4

Day 2

"There are all these moments you think you won't survive. And then you survive."
David Levithan

I was expecting a long drop into a deep lake of ice-cold water. Instead I slid down through the hole on a slide no steeper than the plastic slides on kids's playsets. I land on my rump in waist-deep water. But I sit in shock in that pool of water, noticing first that I'm still alive and need to calm down so the adrenaline will chill out. My limbs feel like they're on fire from the adrenaline burn. Secondly, the water is warm, pretty much room temperature, and then I realize that this new cavern is warm also and substantially brighter.

I'm overwhelmed by all these changes, and the emotions I've been trying to hold in are melting like a slushy left in a car on a hot summer day. I'm trembling from the aftershocks of the adrenaline pumping through me, like a junkie coming down off a high. I was in fight or flight mode; now my body was stuck trying to adjust to the new set of obstacles, the largest of which is the unknown cavern I landed in. The pool of water I'm sitting in is about the size of a swimming pool, but no deeper than a bathtub on my end. The water appears darker in the center where I assume it is much deeper. It has a sandy bottom that helped absorb my fall with slippery rounded rocks on the sides. The water is clear, and I can see to the bottom. I lean back and rinse my hair, pulling it back in a ponytail again. My hair tie stayed in, but my Apple Watch fell off during the fall. Getting the dust and dirt off me makes me feel more energized. I'm feeling better by the minute. Maybe that water I drank had some super restorative mineral in it. I climb out of the pool and sit on a large rock to catch my breath and take in my surroundings. The light is comforting and refreshing, making me realize how much it had been affecting me to have gone without it for so long. I feel like I could breathe again. Like I could survive and maybe even escape.

Only then did the remainder of the cavern come into focus. It reminds me of a scene from a Star Trek episode where a man-eating, cave-dwelling monster is threatening to pop out from behind a rock and attack me. The cavern was alive. There is moss and mushrooms everywhere. Stalactites and stalagmites jutted out randomly while quartz and other minerals glittered. Roots dangled from the ceiling and jutted through the side walls. The ceiling was a high dome of rock and dirt and roots, but there were cracks that let sunlight slip through like the spotlight on a theater stage. The largest of the cracks was directly over the pool I landed in, like a spotlight on the stage of a play. I walk over to a place where sunlight was slicing through and sit in it with my face tilted up absorbing it. As relief coursed through me, the emotions of the day sneak up and I am suddenly ugly crying with tears and snot and screams.

"Why?" I scream over and over like a banshee. "Why?" No one is answering. This trip was supposed to be my reward vacation for my hard work this last year. Why am I being punished? My thoughts agitate in this pattern until I've cried so long that my tears are gone and my nose is runny and stuffed up.

"It's not fair!" I scream at the roots in the ceiling. I'm so exhausted mentally and physically and the angle of the light has moved and is now just a spot in the dome that is slightly less black than the rest of the cavern. Finally warm and dry, I curl up into the fetal position and give into the pull of sleep.

Kevin

People think that the ascent of hiking a mountain is harder than the descent. Honestly they're both hard. The descent can be strenuous too because you are using different muscles than what you use to hike up. Going down requires more quads, and mine are screaming at me right now. The coat is too warm to carry it down, so I leave it behind.

I'm in good physical shape for my age, and my career keeps me active. When Char and I were younger and had more time we would go to the gym together. It was fun to share this time together. Even if we were doing separate exercises, we were together, but now we're not. Last night I slept in a cold tent by myself. It was fun to be cold and snuggle together in a tent when she was with me. I didn't have the energy to start a fire, so I just put on all my clothes and waited for the sun to come up. I wasn't able to sleep. Every time my eyes close I imagine something even more horrific happening to her. I feel like I should've stayed there where she disappeared, but I know logically that I have to get help. It's becoming hard to think clearly when my mind is so clouded with emotion.

The descent is getting less steep as I come to the base of the mountain and prepare to leave Makalu Barun National Park. We picked Mount Pheriche as our hiking destination because it had clearly marked trails. It looked challenging and picturesque. People kept asking us if we were going there to climb Mt. Everest. Heck no, we told them. That takes years to train for, and the survival rate for it is very low. Not my idea of fun, but then again this "advanced" hiking trail hasn't shaped up to be any better.

It's a short walk to our hotel from the base. It's not really a hotel because they don't do the chain hotel thing here like we do in the States. We chose the Pumari Guest House because of its breathtaking views. It advertised cultural immersion among its amenities. The atmosphere feels like going to a relative's house and staying with them. The owners are friendly and attentive to the guests. Meals are communal around the largest dining room table I had ever seen. Char and I enjoyed listening to their stories our first night here.

I grab our packs and walk up to the house. Sita is in the front room putting out refreshments. She waves and calls out, "Hello, Mr. Jones. Where's your pretty wife?" I drop my bags.

"I wish I knew," I tell her with a catch in my voice.

"Oh my goodness," she says with sympathy. "Please come sit. You look like you could fall over right now." She guides me to a wingback chair by the fireplace and then brings me tea and a pastry. "You must tell me everything, Mr Jones."

"It's Kevin, Sita. Please call me Kevin." I run my hand through my hair. "I don't know how to explain this without sounding crazy."

"Trust me, Mr. Kevin, I have heard it all. Tell Sita, and I'll see how I can help."

This is comforting. This lodge is the oldest in the area, and I think that she might actually have seen and heard her fair share of strange occurrences. While she is fit and energetic, her wrinkles and gray hair give away her advanced years.

"Char and I were on the second day of hiking up the advanced trail. We were close to the lookout spot and we couldn't wait to get there and get pictures of the landscape. Char needed a break, so we rested for a minute, and then she went off the trail to go to the bathroom and just disappeared."

"Wait, Mr. Kevin, you went off the trail? You were told very clearly to never leave the trail or designated areas. There is much danger on these mountains. You must describe where you last saw her."

Guilt begins to sink its nasty claws in my chest. Of course it's my fault. I knew better than to let her go off into the bushes, even if it was just to pee.

I give her the mile marker, then describe with as much detail as I can where we stopped. Her eyes widen. She clears her throat. "Mr. Kevin, I don't want to alarm you, but many strange things have happened in that very spot that cannot be explained. I can tell you are worried, and you are right to be so. I'm going to make some calls, and then we need to rally the troops if we are going to have even the slightest chance of finding her, if it's not already too late."

I'm getting very scared. I'm alone in a foreign country, and my wife is missing. This is starting to sound like the beginning of an episode of 60 Minutes. I tell her, "Whatever it takes, anything you need, I'll pay. Just help me bring her back."

Sita nods solemnly. "No promises, Mr. Kevin. I have a book I think you need to read. You have studied cultures all over the world and know that many have strange stories and beliefs. This mountain was worshiped by the Plesdibu people thousands of years ago. They have tales about people disappearing on the mountain, much like your Charlotte."

Sita pulls a worn book from a shelf above the fireplace called <u>The Rise and Demise of the Plesdibu</u>. The scientist in me is fascinated, but the husband is scared to open it. I nod thanks.

"You go rest in your room and let Sita get things arranged. I'll come get you when I know more." She heads to the front desk and pulls out a binder full of emergency numbers, I assume. I have nothing left to do but go to my empty room and imagine all the horrible scenarios Charlotte could be in, each more gruesome. It's so routine to unlock the door and throw the gear inside that the blast of her perfume hits me without warning. I wasn't prepared for that. I have to get in the room before I have a mental breakdown in the hallway. Once in my room I collapse on my bed. I feel too guilty to sleep but my body is literally shutting down from exhaustion. It helps to know that I have help.

I wake up from a nap when the absolute worst thought comes to me. I have to call her parents and work to tell them what is going on. I don't want to, but I know I should. This will not be fun. I have to go to the front desk to use the phone, and Sita is there, which makes me feel better.

"Sita, I need to make some phone calls to Charlotte's family and work and let them know what's going on."

"Oh no, Mr. Kevin. I wouldn't do that quite yet. Give it a few days, and if she isn't found before your trip is over, then you call. No need to worry them now when there's nothing they can do about it."

This is a huge relief, and I see the wisdom in it. I ask her a question that has been bothering me all day. "Sita, do you believe that this could have been something supernatural? You can answer honestly. I'm an archaeologist, so any answer won't shock me."

"Mr. Kevin, I'm one hundred percent certain this is a spiritual battle and the number one person she has to fight is herself. The battle will be in her mind and emotions. Do you pray, Mr. Kevin?"

I look down at my feet. "I used to, but life got busy, and things have been good for me and my career, so to be perfectly honest, I didn't pray because I haven't needed him lately. I'm ashamed to admit that. He probably won't answer my prayers since I've ignored him so long."

She pats my arm with a wink. "God isn't like us—He doesn't hold grudges. I think now would be a good time to start praying. Now go rest and read that book. And pray."

Chapter 5

Day 3

"Hard times don't create heroes. It is during the hard times when the 'hero' within us is revealed."
Bob Riley

I was never a sound sleeper. I had to get up too many times for the bathroom and to let the dogs out when we still had dogs, so for me to sleep all night uninterrupted was and is a strange occurrence. I sit straight up, wide awake, disoriented, like when you stay in a strange hotel. "It's real," I whisper. I had subconsciously hoped that when I woke up it would have all been a bad dream. Twisting my torso left and right, I crack my back then do a few neck rolls to work out the stiffness. I will never take my memory foam mattress for granted ever again.

The sunlight is filtering through the cracks, angling to the right now instead of the left like last night. I was unable yesterday, physically or mentally, to explore this cavern and take inventory of what resources are available. But first I go to the pool and get a long drink of water. It tastes like that expensive mineral water you can buy at the supermarket that comes out of a waterfall on an island somewhere. I thought it was a gimmick for advertising, but this tastes identical. The metallic mineral aftertaste is refreshing and thirst-quenching.

From what I can make out, the cavern is the size of a small house, but the areas that are shaded could be bigger or smaller. I head to the right side of it to make use of the morning sun while it is shining there. There are many rocks and cracks and stalagmites to navigate around, so I have to watch where I step carefully. When I reach the farthest edge of the cavern, I am not prepared for the surprise on the far wall. In faded red, gold, black and white paint is an ancient cave mural.

Kevin is an archeologist and while I support his career and passion for ancient remains and rocks, I don't share his enthusiasm. But I have been forced to listen to many lectures on new archeological discoveries around the world. I recall hearing about caves with paintings in western Europe dating clear back to prehistoric times and that most paintings are in caves that are extremely difficult to access. This cave certainly fits that category.

Now that I know what is on this cave wall, I step back a few paces to take in the whole painting. There are several types of symbols and drawings spanning approximately twelve feet wide by three feet high. The colors are faded reds, yellow, black, and white. The paintings depict humans, animals, and plants in scenes of hunting, gathering and worship. I think about how much Kevin would have wanted to see this and how important it would have been to him. This sudden thought about him brings a wave of sorrow so sharp, taking my breath away.

"Kev, I wish you were here to see this," I whisper to the cave wall and swipe away a treacherous tear.

Next I get closer to examine each section of the paintings more closely. At the left I see humans herding goats up a mountain, and then they fall into a cave. They drink from the waterfall and eat mushrooms, bulbous roots of tall grasses, and berries. Then it shows them worshipping a god that lives in the waterfall. It provides their food, water and nourishment. The last section shows a hole in the cave and them escaping. These ancient humans have left a roadmap for surviving and potentially escaping this cave. Between the sunlight and the paintings I feel hope, and it's not a minute too late because my empty stomach is signaling its displeasure with tomcat-worthy growls.

Before I look for the foods in the paintings, I need to examine the rest of the cave while the sun is shining on those areas. The sunlight is shining straight into the cave and it reflects the water everywhere, creating a kaleidoscope of diamonds on the walls, ceiling and floor. It was magical, and I could see why ancient humans would worship it. The waterfall was alive in a riot of reflected light and color but also living with life-giving plants around it. The paintings showed a tall grass by the cave that people were eating the tuber and roots of. I pull one stalk up, making sure to get the roots also. It comes out easily due to the moist soil near the pool. After rinsing it off in the water, I give it a skeptical sniff. It has a strong smell like a wild onion and resembles one too. I peel off the roots from the bulb and nibble the bottom. It squirts juices as I bite into it and has a similar onion taste but is milder and sweeter. I finish the bulb and wonder if the grassy stem is edible like a chive. The stem is hollow like a chive, so I eat it as well. My stomach was empty before I ate these and I worry about how it will react to this new food, so I only eat two wild onions, as I have named them. I scoop up a couple mouthfuls of water then follow the light through the remainder of the cave.

The fading sunlight slants through the cracks to the left again like last night. After seeing the waterfall and the cave paintings, I guess I was expecting something wonderful, but I was underwhelmed by a pile of rocks beside the wall of the cave. It looked like there had been a rockslide. Based on the paintings, this could be where they escaped. As I examine the rocks and climb over them, I theorize that thousands of years ago an earthquake could have caused a crack or hole in the top or side of this cave, which could have been when they found the cave. Continued aftershocks may have caused a rockslide trapping them, but future earth-quakes and rockslides allowed them to escape. The finality of the giant pile of rocks is a bucket of cold water to the positive discoveries I found earlier in the cave today. I am suddenly exhausted and can't take any more emotional highs and lows.

I return to the pool and stare into its calm silvery surface. As hopeful as I was about finding food and a possible escape route, the pile of rocks is a real, physical representation of my entrapment. My chest gets tight and I try to massage the pain away. Knowing all too well what this feeling is leading up to, I try very hard to calm down. I don't want to give in to the depression of this situation, but it is sucking me in like a black hole, and I don't have the physical or mental energy to fight its gravitational pull. I find a mossy flat area by the pool that I can lie down on. I'm emotionally drained and need to shut down before I'm triggered any further. Closing my eyes and breathing slowly, I let sleep wash over me, praying a short nap will help me reset.

"Charlotte," a still, small voice whispers. "Charlotte," the voice says again. I sit up and see the sun is directly overhead. I was asleep a long time, and now I only have a few hours of sunlight left coming through cracks. My stomach grumbles loudly, but I get a few handfuls of water first before eating. The wild onions stayed down ok this morning, so this afternoon I eat two. I am going to try another food from the painting. This plant looks similar to watercress that I've seen in the produce section. I think it might be part of the mustard greens family. It grows in clusters in the shallow water with small, rounded leaves that grow in. It's a delicate plant used in many of those ten-dollar salads you see in fancy restaurants. I reach out into the pool and grab a handful of the watercress by the stems, and they pull up easily. I place them on a rock beside me and examine the stems and leaves for dirt. They all look healthy and bright green, and I fold two and eat them whole. They have a slight crunch then a peppery taste, very similar to mustard greens. This is tasty, but light so I finish off the rest of my handful. Now that I have food in my belly, I'm tired again. Trauma is an energy sucker. My body is still processing the trauma from the previous few days and healing physically and mentally. I decide to call it a night since the light has mostly left the cave. Tomorrow I can explore more.

Kevin

I read the book cover to cover last night. I knew I wouldn't be able to sleep anyways. If I wasn't an archaeologist, I wouldn't believe any of this was possible The book claims that the Plesdibu people were descended from ancient Egyptian slaves. They worked engraving hieroglyphs and painting murals in the tombs under the pyramids of Giza. A burial chamber deep below the pyramids collapsed, killing many of their fellow workers. They methodically planned an escape out of Egypt, up the Nile, then across the desert and onto the Asian continent. During their enslavement they had heard traders and nomadic peoples tell about mountains so high that they reached into the clouds. The gods lived there and granted miracles to those who climbed up to their highest points and drank from the healing waters. On they trekked until they arrived in these mountains. They made homes at the base of the mountain but would make annual trips up the mountain to offer sacrifices to the gods and drink the magical water of the pool in the cave.

But the mountain didn't give up its secrets without a challenge. Every month the magnetic force of the full moon is at its strongest and it pulls open the doors of the cave and allows entrance or exit for just a few moments. Visitors are warned to be quick when visiting so that they are not trapped in the cave for another month. The full moon is the only day the doors open. There is no other exit.

The Plesdibus left intricate cave paintings using the artistry they learned in Egypt. Visitors are warned in the murals about the cave and its monthly cycle. Many locals in recent times consider these stories to be made up, but there have been too many strange occurrences to disregard them. People have been reported to disappear and reappear a month or even several months later. They are unable to express what they have seen and experienced while there. Any sicknesses, diseases and even deformities are completely healed permanently. This legend has been a tightly guarded secret from the outside world. If modern science or medicine discovered this, it would corrupt and abuse this holy place.

I read the book and reread it until Sita knocks on my door. I must look shocked. "It looks like you read the book, Mr. Kevin." I just nod. "I've seen that look on every face that has read that book. People either mock or marvel."

"I've studied lots of places and cultures, but this one takes the cake," I whisper.

"Well, I don't know what cake it took, but many people have trouble trusting what they cannot see," Sita replies. "But I think you've had a close enough encounter to believe it. There's a whole world out there that we can't explain. I know you are scared for your Charlotte, but maybe it would help if you could imagine that she is having the adventure of a lifetime."

Chapter 6

Day 4

"*We cannot control the things that happen to us, but we can control our reactions to them.*"
Epictetus

Something tickles my nose, and I swat at my face. And now I'm awake. A patch of springy moss has made an adequate pillow for my situation. After stretching, I roll over onto all fours and stand carefully. I feel more rested, and my head is clearer too. My situation and setting come back to me quicker than the previous ones. I have an initial wave of anxiety about my situation, but curiosity is running a close second. First things first, I go to the pool and splash my face and take a long drink. With a big sigh I look around and start making a mental list of what I need to do today. Lists have always helped me focus my time and energy, and now more than ever they may keep me from going insane.

First, I need to identify all the tasks that need to be done then prioritize them. This is much easier with a pencil and paper, lots of sticky notes and some Sharpies too. If I was in a meeting at work, we would have a big dry erase board for brainstorming. I hoped I could find something to write on the cave walls with, but everything I pick up and press to the rock surface crumbles. The ground near the pool is dusty clay. With no other options I bend down and make a line with my finger. It makes a legible mark, like writing with your finger in flour on the kitchen counter. I find a large flat section of floor in the middle of the cave where I will have the most light throughout the day. With my finger, I write "Needs" and underline it, making bullet points underneath. Water goes first then food and protection. I put check marks beside water and food and just that small symbol is comforting. It's not lost on me that I have the base needs of Maslow's pyramid; all of my basic needs are met. Beside food I also draw a question mark. I draw an arrow off to the right and write "limited" and "not sustainable" and "nutritious"?

Protection gets a question mark. This hasn't been much of a concern until now that I actually think about it. I draw two arrows to the right and write: weather and predators. Beside predators I have more arrows with insects, spiders, rodents, and larger predators. I'm too scared to write down the words "cats" or "bears." I have enough things to worry about without adding on fearing the unknown. Kevin worked in many places that were potentially unsafe, and I would be more scared for him than he was. He would tell me that he views it as an adventure, an opportunity for a great story afterwards. He liked the famous quote from an unknown author, "Replace fear of the unknown with curiosity," but I would counter that with "Curiosity killed the cat." Thus we would dance around the issue, with the end result being him going and me staying where it was safe. I had so many opportunities to travel with him that I never took him up on, and I regret them all. Those trips now seem tame compared to my current setting. I vow to never waste another chance at an adventure with him. Hopefully I get that chance.

I continue writing on the floor, having to work around rocks and occasional stalagmites and write down all the facts I can remember. I've read survival stories of people who were trapped or stranded for long periods of time who eventually forgot their previous lives and lost track of time and ultimately their sanity. As stupid as it feels, I start a column labeled "Facts."

I start with my full name, address, birthday and even social security number. I put Kevin's name and information. Next I list the date of my accident and the events leading up to it. Then farther away I start the typical tally chart for how many days I've been in this cave, and I make four hash marks.

The mental exhaustion of my situation drains my energy. After returning to the pool and eating a meal of watercress and wild onions, I feel exhausted. I go back to my mossy bed and succumb to the numbing power of sleep to finish off the day.

Kevin

Sita's husband Pelo has rounded up a group of rugged, weather-worn men for a search team. There is a pile of gear in the front room. Backpacks, walking sticks, hiking shoes and boots, water canteens, large knives similar to machetes, and a few guns. This is not a pleasure stroll. We need to be prepared for any possible scenario. Charlotte could be hurt somewhere or kidnapped by outlaws for ransom or even attacked by a wild animal. The task of finding and rescuing her has been beyond what my brain could process. Seeing that people are organized and have a plan is reassuring.

Pelo calls everyone to gather round. We will be in three groups of two and are told to never go off alone. One person in each pair has a weapon, and the other carries the first aid supplies and tent. We have walkie-talkies to check in with the other groups every thirty minutes even if there is no news. Sita will have one at the lodge and be monitoring everyone's progress and relaying information as needed. A backup team is on standby at the lodge for emergencies. Pelo rolls out a topographical map onto the dining room table and weighs the corners down with teacups. "We are here," he says, pointing to the base of the mountain. He traces his finger up the line of the trail on the mountainside and points. "This is approximately where Kevin last saw Charlotte."

I nod and swallow a lump in my throat. I am nervous that these big burly mountain men somehow think less of me for "losing" my wife, but I see only compassion on their faces. Pelo slaps a meaty hand on my shoulder. "It could happen to anyone. These are dangerous places and things happen here that sometimes cannot be explained." The other men look around at each other with raised eyebrows, like kids trying to keep a secret. "It's ok, guys, Sita gave him the book, and he has a background in studying weird ancient stuff."

"Weird ancient stuff" would be a funny definition for students in my next lecture. It's actually a fairly accurate description, especially for outsiders of our discipline. Anthropologists and historians study ancient people and cultures, yet we typically view what we discover through the lens of our own modern culture. I need to look at this situation without my Western-based ideologies. Pelo continues directing the group while I am having internal philosophical arguments.

"Here's the plan. Group one is Nakul and Ram; you will go east when we get to the spot where she disappeared. Group two will be Kevin and me. We will go north, up the mountain. And group three, heading west around the mountain, will be Arav and Ruva. We will head up the trail together, with groups one and three one hundred feet left and right of the trail. The goal is to cover the trip up the mountain slowly in case she came down. Report anything that is not part of the natural environment." He looks around at all of us and nods.

"Let's pray before you boys head out," Sita says, grabbing Pelo's hand and mine, making a circle. "Kevin, will you lead us?"

"Geesh, I'm a little rusty." I shuffle my feet. "Would you pray, Pelo?"

He nods. "Lord, thank you for this day and bringing all of us together, even though it was through these tough circumstances. We know you are all-seeing and all-knowing and everywhere all at once. Guide our eyes and ears and feet. Protect us from harm. And most of all, give Charlotte peace right now; help her to hold on to hope and have faith that You will take care of her. We love you, Jesus, and can't wait to tell this story and give you the glory for answering our prayers and rescuing Charlotte. Thank you in advance." He pauses, and all the men say, "Amen," and start clapping like in a sports huddle. Their positive spirit is amazing and inspiring. I whisper a silent prayer for God to help me to trust Him through all this.

"Let's head out!" Pelo announces.

"Channel one on the walkie-talkies, boys," Sita announces over the hubbub. Everyone grabs their packs and turns their walkie-talkies on. We each give Sita a hug goodbye, but Pelo dips her, giving her a big smooch. "Something to remember me by," he chuckles and winks. Turning back to the group, "Ok, time to get serious. Let's go. We will pause for a break in two hours." And with that the search begins.

Chapter 7

Day 5

Waking up with regret is a miserable way to start the day. I'm regretting yesterday's decision to do nothing, both physically and emotionally. As tempting as closing my eyes again into nothingness is, my mother's voice is screaming at me in my head to get up and stop being a lazy bum. I'm ashamed to admit that last night I went to sleep hoping that when I closed my eyes I just wouldn't wake up. Upon waking I discover that I actually do want to live. My life right now feels more painful than death, as sick as that sounds.

I've attempted suicide twice before in my life. I know the sinking, sucking feeling of it pulling you, of hoping that escaping life will end the pain. I have heard many people criticize and talk down about those who have killed themselves. They criticize the person for being selfish and cannot understand how one could do that. However, every individual I have been around who has attempted it was in an excruciating amount of mental anguish, emotional trauma, or physical pain. My heart breaks for them. When I held a knife to my wrist and a bottle of pills to my mouth, the only thing that kept me from dying was thinking of Kevin and my family. I could not imagine the horror of one of them coming into my home and finding me dead on the floor. I couldn't do that to them. The future pain that I would cause others, in my mind, was greater than the pain I was currently in.

I am stiff from being curled up in the fetal position for hours on a bed of moss. I roll off my side onto all fours and come up into the tabletop position. I arch my back and curve it down several times for the cat-cow yoga pose. I go down into a plank and hold it, counting to thirty, before I lean back into downward dog. I continue my yoga stretches, trying to clear my mind and just focus on the feeling of stretching my muscles. As I come into my final pose and bring my hands to my heart, I whisper "Namaste" and exhale until there is no more air in my lungs. I stay there breathing slowly. Then I raise my arms straight up in the sun salutation, and for the first time in ages, I say, "Thank you, Lord, for a new day."

Seated with my legs folded under me, I allow God's peace to fill me. I feel deeply convicted for not asking him for help. I'm a strong, successful, independent woman. Independence is great, but we were created to be dependent on God. He's not domineering; he wants a partnership, a relationship. Since no one is here to hear me, I pray out loud and ask God for his help. My brain is screaming that I'm literally talking to the walls of the cave, but it wouldn't be the first time I was accused of talking to someone who wasn't there.

"God, I believe that you are out there somewhere, and I believe that you are here with me now. I'm sorry that I haven't asked you for help in this situation. Forgive me for not looking to you for help first. I don't know what happened to bring me where I am now; in fact, I don't even know where "where" is. But I know that you are big, and you've got the whole world in your hands literally. I ask you, Lord, to send help, to guide rescuers or someone, anyone, to rescue me. While I wait for them, Lord, help me to stay alive. Show me how to survive in this place that you created. You didn't allow this to happen just for me to die here, so that means you have a purpose for it, and I trust you in that. I pray that after I've been rescued and returned to my normal life that this experience will have changed me for the better. I will give you all the glory for it. I ask this all in Jesus' name, and I thank you for it already. Amen."

My imagination is coming up with fantastical scenarios for how God is going to help me. I'd love to report that something miraculous happened after that prayer like Moses parting the Red Sea or ravens bringing Elijah food during the drought. Nothing changed. Except me. My attitude shifted from depression and complaining to feeling hopeful, energetic, and even excited to see how this story was going to play out. This was going to make for an awesome testimony! God was getting ready to show off big time. I heard it explained once that God is like John Wayne. He's a big, tall cowboy with broad shoulders and the fastest on the draw. He loves to rescue people who are hurt and broken. He seeks them out, kills the bad guy, and rides off into the sunset with them.

I take the good vibes my prayer gave me and use it to start my day. I need to get into a rhythm and routine because I don't have much daylight, and I am working under some serious time limits and constraints to figuring out how to survive here. At home, I can't function in the morning until I'm dressed with my hair and makeup done. I'm not a diva; I just don't feel ready to start the day without that. I'm not able to do those things now, but I can wash my face and freshen up to stay as clean as my situation will allow me. My clothes feel greasy, so I will put laundry on my to-do list.

I think back to when I was in my twenties and things were simpler. I would drink my morning coffee and read my Bible every morning with the dogs curled up next to me on the couch. Now I'm too busy to have dogs, and I take my coffee to go, always in a rush, without a thought for God or prayer. And I wonder why I'm stressed and don't have peace. Without a Starbucks here, the best I can do is drink some water and meditate out loud on the scriptures I memorized years ago. Today I will pray and meditate on the Lord's Prayer.

Feeling a bit more normal, I look for some greens for breakfast. Gathering and identifying food will be a big job for later, but for now I'm just looking for a small amount to start my day. I have noticed that I'm not as hungry as I was a few days ago. I guess my body is getting used to eating less, which will be a big help. I've always been petite but with the appetite of a lumberjack. With a handful of what I am now calling water lettuce, I go over to my lists, sit down in front of them and think. A big danger presently is allowing my emotions to keep me from making rational decisions and planning for the future. It's overwhelming looking at everything I wrote down yesterday, but it also gives the fear and anxiety of the situation boundaries. There is a finite number of obstacles to overcome, so every day I survive, I am making that list shorter. Everything I can think of is written down, and giving those things a name and forming a plan makes me feel a little bit more in control.

I'm sitting here next to the pool minding my own business and munching on breakfast. My brain is evaluating which item is most important to address first, when I hear a sound. Things have been so quiet for so many days, with my movements being the only sound other than the stream and the pool that this new sound startles me. I freeze and slowly look around for the source. It almost sounded like a non-distinct voice that you could hear from a distance but not be able to tell what they were saying. It was a low moan like the foghorn of a tugboat on a humid summer night. Protection just jumped up in priority after hearing that sound. Logically, I know that it is probably wind blowing through various tunnels in the mountain, but it sounded like someone was hurt, like a man who was in pain. This sets my mind racing: if I'm injured down inside this mountain, could other people have fallen too? I haven't fully explored my cave, but now I see that I need to search it carefully to look for anyone else who could've been hurt or other potential dangers. I need to assess how safe I am and how I can, if possible at all, protect myself.

I decide I need to wait a while to listen for it again. I stay perfectly still and close my eyes. I start counting in my head and hear the sound again before I hit ninety. It's louder again, but most likely only because I'm paying attention to it this time. I keep my eyes closed and focus on which direction it's coming from. I came in on the stream that flows into the pool, but the sound doesn't seem like it's coming from that direction. It's coming from the far side of the cavern with all the stalactites. I haven't explored there much because of how uneven and rocky it is. And drippy. But maybe there is something over there that I missed. I hear the sound again and have convinced myself it's nothing lethal, but maybe it could be a sign for a way out. They always say to follow the fresh air, like Gandalf down in the mines of Moria in <u>Lord of the Rings</u>. I shake my head because I feel ridiculous thinking about fantasy novels while I'm trapped underground. But fantasy has been my favorite book genre since reading <u>The Chronicles of Narnia</u> as a kid because the characters are always on a quest or off on a great adventure. I wish in a way that ten-year-old me, who loved reading about dragons and elves, could see me now living in a cave. She would flip.

The side of the cave the sound is coming from won't get sunlight till after noon, so I have a little time now to think about protection. My initial thought was to make some type of barricade around where I sleep, like a rock fence, but there are very few rocks small enough for me to move and any predator would be able to easily jump over my primitive barriers. Thus, protection in the form of fencing or barricades is out. That leaves making an alarm system to notify me of a potential attack, much like ADT when a burglar breaks into your house. I decide to use some smaller gravel-sized rocks from beside the pool. I step on one and it makes a nice scratchy sound, like a car pulling into a gravel driveway. A few handful of these around my sleeping pallet just might give me an extra second to react to a potential threat. I get a couple handfuls of them and sprinkle them around my bed. This little action makes me feel some small form of accomplishment. I am not completely defenseless anymore.

The sun is overhead, and now I can see into the far corner of the cave where I heard the sound earlier. It is still randomly floating on invisible currents like pollen on a windy spring day. I'm worried about losing track of time and potentially getting injured or lost if I'm not back before it gets dark. This section has a rough, foreign geography. I grab some sand from the pool to sprinkle on my exploration. It is a lighter color than the floor of the cave and should help me find my way back if I get turned around. I start to weave through the stalagmites, which are tall and conical. Some are short, in the early stages of forming, while many others are taller than I am, even some reaching to the top of the cave. The stalactites hanging down are also ominous and dangerous looking, like being inside of a shark's mouth. I feel like one could fall and impale me if I make too loud of a sound. They are extraordinarily fragile despite their menacing appearance. Kevin showed me once on a trip that they can break with just the lightest touch. A stalactite only grows a few inches every thousand years, so this is the rocky equivalent to walking through the Redwood National Park. I take small steps as I navigate around them, remembering to sprinkle sand every few yards. I'm not quite sure which direction to walk through this rock forest, but the sound seemed to be coming from the far corner, of course. Back by the pool I couldn't see the corner because their height and density blocked my view.

I am being dripped on by the stalactites constantly, making everything damp. It's these drips that have mineral deposits, which create the cones. I know not to touch them because the oil on my hands could cause them to stop growing. I know I started counting my steps when I entered. The dim light makes navigating very difficult, which makes accurately estimating how far this end of the cave is from my pool problematic. I dance around a very large stalagmite and notice that the ones ahead are starting to get smaller. Some are connected top and bottom, making a column. In fact, it looks like the ceiling is starting to slope towards the floor about thirty yards ahead. I pause and look around. I cannot see the pool from here. I drop my last little bit of sand by my feet. There are fewer rocks here, but the ground is rough with smaller gravel-sized rocks. I slide a foot forward tentatively before putting weight on it and repeat carefully as I walk toward the wall of the cave.

As I come up to the wall, I notice that it is much different from the painted wall. It's not tall and flat but arched like the edge of a dome. I feel the sloped wall, and it is cool and damp but not smooth. There are lots of cracks and veins in the rock. Then I feel a small puff of air. It is cool and fresh. I forgot how great fresh air smelled until this moment, like new life. It's crisp like the first sip of a can of Sprite. I follow my hands down the wall until I feel the crack the air is coming in through. I place my hand over it, but nothing is coming out now. I follow the crack with my fingers; it is wider at the bottom and then travels up over my head. I assume this crack was made by the mountain shifting or an earthquake. I'm exploring the rock around the crack when I hear a high, quiet whistle like a tea kettle but softer. It is accompanied by a tiny wisp of wind through the crack, seemingly near the smaller end. Then with more speed the wind blows through the bottom end with a louder, low moan. I bend down on all fours and feel around the big end of the crack. Some areas of it are wider and I can stick my fist into it but then it narrows as it goes up. I don't see any light coming through or hear anything other than wind. However, this is an interesting development.

I don't know what else I can do at the moment, so I turn around to head back to the pool. There is still a small amount of light, but I am glad I have the trail of white sand to follow. I carefully travel back to my pool and experience that feeling you get when coming home. It's just a pool with a pallet of moss, but it's everything to me. I'm tired from my excursions today, so I eat more water lettuce and some mushrooms. After a big drink of water, I nestle down in my moss and think about what I discovered today and what it could mean for me. I wonder as I fall asleep if Kevin misses me like I miss him.

Kevin

I don't know why I thought this trip would be faster and easier than my first one with Charlotte. A search this intense makes for a slower trip up the mountain. The groups going beside the trail had to carefully hike through dense forest and navigate large rocks and boulders left behind from rockslides and avalanches. Pelo and I had the easier hike on the trail and took over carrying all the gear for the other men. We scanned the trail before taking any steps forward to look for tracks and evidence of anyone coming down the mountain. Sita and Pelo said that no one else had hiked up the mountain since Charlotte and I. Hikers have to sign in and out at the lodge before accessing the trail behind it. This has helped the Park many times to find hurt and lost guests.

Yesterday we had hoped to make it to where Charlotte and I camped after our first day hiking. We stopped about a third of the way up the mountain and camped a short way off the trail under a canopy of pine trees. Arav got a big fire going to heat our food and keep predators away. I guess it's the archaeologist in me, but I'm always curious about the folklore and history of other cultures. Some good campfire stories will help pass the time, and maybe I'll learn something useful.

"Tell me about the history of your people and this mountain," I ask the group around the campfire.

They look around at each other and all point simultaneously to Pelo. He chuckles and takes a drink before speaking. "I don't have a fancy degree on my wall," he winks at me, "but I do consider myself an amateur historian. After our people migrated here, they made a home at the base of these mountains. They originally moved up here from various places long ago to avoid slavery, persecution and war. We were oppressed and hunted for worshiping the one true God. This spot is ideal because there is only one way in and out of our villages, so we can defend it better against enemies. We do not want to be cut off from the world like the Amish in your country. We just want to be able to live the way we want without people telling us what to do."

I let out a quiet whistle. "Wow. That is quite fascinating. Thank you for sharing. I'd love to hear more. Oral history tells as much or more about your people and values as any history textbook could," I reply. They told other old tales about mythical creatures like the Yeti that prowled the mountains and lived in caves. They were feared to be aggressive and attack any who dared climb these mountains, so some in the past have left sacrifices for them to appease their thirst for blood and violence.

We left at first light, wanting to make it to the halfway point today. Each step gets more difficult due to the oxygen levels decreasing and temperature dropping. The trail is clear, but the undergrowth of the forest is dense, rocky and impassable in some places. There hasn't been any rain or snow in several days, so my footprints coming down are visible, but they obscure our prints going up. Our best hope is that Charlotte just got disoriented after her jump and wandered away from the trail only to get lost in the thick pine forest.

After a few hours hiking this morning, we arrive at where Charlotte and I camped. This location is recommended by the Park as it is the break in the two-day hike up the mountain. It is obvious that people, us, camped here recently: a fire pit with fresh charcoal, a broken bungee cord and Charlotte's jacket, which I left behind in my haste to get down the mountain for help. I forgot that it had been warm and sunny that morning and she had taken off her jacket, which means that wherever she is now she only has on her hiking pants and a flannel shirt. The weather is unpredictable, going from sunny and warm in the afternoon to below freezing at night.

Pelo sees me clutching the jacket, holding it close. It still smells like her, vanilla and cherry from her lotion. He tells me, "Just because her jacket is here doesn't mean that she's gone. In fact it's a clue. Let's look around a bit more then follow her tracks."

Other than some waste there are no other clues. We take a break before starting on the second part of the day. I'm simultaneously eager to get moving and terrified. What if what I saw isn't there anymore and they think I'm crazy or hallucinating? I remind myself that they believed my story so far without hesitation or doubts. Our Cliff Bar and water break pep us up to explore more and keep moving; we need to get as much done as humanly possible before the sun goes down.

We hike around the sides of the rock she jumped off so as to not disturb her tracks and whatever else is there. I point to the ground just past the rock. "Right there is where I found her watch."

Pelo bends down to ground level and examines the dirt. He and Nakul look around the entire area, then get large sticks, which they use to tap and poke the churned-up dirt with. Nothing but plain old dirt so far. I'm holding my breath, so scared that at any moment the ground will suddenly cave in and suck us all in. Pelo stands up and takes his walking stick with both hands and raises it high, striking straight down into the dirt. It sinks in but only a few inches before coming to a cracking stop. He repeats this every few inches around the loose dirt.

"I have a suspicion, but there's only one way to test it," Pelo says. "Ram, please hand me that hand trowel we packed." He gets down on his knees and starts to scoop away the loose dirt, making a circular shape. As he shoves the trowel down, you can hear a scraping sound. As he continues going it is evident what he is hitting. Just a few feet under the loose dirt that I suspected Charlotte fell into is a layer of solid rock. He widens the area to reveal solid granite rock.

"No, no, no, no, no," I mumble. "She was right here; I know it." My hands are shaking and I'm seeing spots. I might pass out and that would be embarrassing.

I must make a sound because Pelo looks at me with compassion. "Just because this is a dead end doesn't mean we won't find her. There's still a lot of area to search." He looks up at the sky, noting that the sun is close to setting. "We won't get anything else done tonight, so let's set up camp and make a plan for to-morrow."

The others wrap their arms around me, helping me walk back to the clearing. I don't think I would've made it there without them. They warm up cans of food for dinner, but I can't eat. I just curl up in my tent, still shaking and terrified. I hope God can hear the silent prayers of my heart because right now I can't find the words.

Chapter 8

Day 6

There's no alarm clock or environmental sounds in the cave except for the constant dripping and the occasional wind blowing through the cracks. I don't even hear the dripping anymore. It's like people who have lived by a train their whole lives who don't even notice the train when it goes by. I've never been great with silence. I've been told that it wasn't healthy because it was partially about me avoiding my thoughts and issues. I would jokingly reply that it drowned out the other voices in my head. This, however, can get you in trouble if you say that to the wrong person. Without sounds or clocks, dogs or people and their inevitable noises, the only thing to wake me up is my body feeling rested. How novel! When was the last time, or have I ever, slept until my body naturally woke up on its own? I had caffeine headaches the first couple days after landing in this cave, but I feel like I've been detoxed from it and other addictive substances like salt and sugar. I can already see a big improvement. My stomach is flatter, and even though I had diarrhea the second and third days, now I am significantly less bloated. It occurs to me what a waste it is for me to lose a few pounds with no one here to see it.

I remember that I need to start every day by being thankful. Feeling sorry for myself is completely counterproductive in my situation or in any situation. I heard a preacher say once that if the only prayer you ever pray is "Thank you, Jesus," it would be enough. I sit up and cross my legs, and even though no one is around me, I bow my head. I like to start off my prayers by telling God what I'm thankful for: I'm thankful that I woke up this morning and even though my circumstances are bleak, I thank him for providing for me. Then I ask him to help me to appreciate his gifts and give me wisdom to know how to use them. I thank him for Kevin and ask God to comfort him because I am sure he is a mess. I thank him for my parents, for their example to me, and I ask Him to forgive me for all the heartache I put them through in my younger years. I thank him for my nieces and nephews and that he would be with them and guide them as they grow up. I take a minute to let the enormity of how blessed my life has been sink in. It is not lost on me that everything I have thanked him for has been people, not things. My salary doesn't matter anymore. My designer clothes, purses and shoes or 401k don't matter. For all I know, I will never see those things again, and I'm not bothered by that one bit. This is new for me, basing my happiness on being reunited with Kevin and my family as opposed to money, status, cars, and my career.

I ask God to guide my day. I tell him that I can't do this without his help. I am completely reliant on his grace and provision, which I don't like, and I tell him that too. Admitting that I want to be god of my life and have full control is hard but liberating. Trying to be god is exhausting. Failure is inevitable and absolute. Life happens, and you realize that the little control you thought you had on your life was just an illusion. But I remember the scripture "My grace is sufficient for you for my power is made perfect in weakness." Grace was always one of those church words that was confusing because I didn't know what it meant. I think it must have been one of those King James words that now nobody knows really what it means. Suddenly, I know what it means; I can feel what it means. Grace means that God helps me do what I can't do on my own without earning his help. It's undeserved. God helps me because he is good.

With this encouragement, I get up from my morning meditation and go to the pool. I splash my face and get a drink. I go to get my breakfast and have a remarkable discovery. The areas that I have eaten from have regrown. In fact, I can't tell where I have eaten anything from in or around the pool. I whisper, "This can't be real." I rubbed my eyes and opened them again and it's still the same. The only word for this is "miracle." God is providing for me in this cave miraculously. He is taking care of me. I fall to my knees and weep in joy and humility. His kindness and provision have pierced my heart so sweetly. I was praying and believing and trusting, but there's always that one small part that's still doubting, wondering "What if?" But thankfully, God is bigger than my fears. I'm not going to starve. I'm not going to die. This is a dire situation, but God is taking care of me in the middle of it. I will either find my way out or be rescued, but I will not die here.

I'm just sitting here staring at the greens, minding my own business and thinking, "This is a miracle." The Bible is filled with stories of miracles, and I've heard people give testimonies about them, but most of them were overseas. I'm staring at one right now; I'm eating one right now. Physically. I can touch a miracle. My brain speculates in doubt that it could be an optical illusion, but when I take a bite, they are real and crunchy. The mushrooms are bigger, and the greens are sweeter. My morning meal is joyful, and I thank God for his provision again.

I need to get my day moving or else I will lose the light. I start back again where the cave paintings are. Now that I know there are cracks, fissures, and a hole according to the paintings, I wonder if the people who came here long ago used any of them for coming and going. I study the paintings trying to determine if there is a flow or if they are all just random pictures and symbols. Starting on the right is a cluster of hand silhouettes and animals. Then there is a large circular doorway with a cave that has a waterfall and large pool. The hands and animals are drawn beside the pool. Finally, there is another doorway but on the opposite side of the cave and it is like a large crack instead of a traditional cave opening. Then there are more handprints and animals. The moon is prominent in the drawings. Kevin has travelled the world studying these paintings, and I have learned a lot about them, sometimes unwillingly, by osmosis. I cautiously touch a small spot of the painting. It rubs on my fingers like charcoal and I would assume the red is from ochre. Neither of these things are naturally occurring in the cave, so these people would have brought them with them.

I've been around the cave several times throughout the last several days, and I haven't seen any bones. Bones don't decay, so if people and animals had been in here then none of them died in here. Due to the difficulty of entering and exiting the cave, it is highly unlikely that even if an animal or person died a scavenger took any of them out of the cave. This realization gives me hope. No one has ever died in here.

I'm examining the details of the paintings when I notice that in the drawing of the cave there are small vertical lines under the drawing of the pool. The first and last parts don't have any. I wonder if this was a way of keeping track of how many days they were in the cave or just decorative. I decide to count the dashes, twenty-eight. Early peoples based their calendars on the phases of the moon. A month in the lunar calendar is twenty-eight days. That's not a random number. It's a sign from God to give me hope and purpose. God doesn't have accidents; everything he does is on purpose and has purpose; even the things we mess up, he purposely retools them for our good. God guided the hands of these ancient people hundreds of years ago is to guide and direct me. The volume of God's foresight and provision is mind-blowing.

It looked like the people around the cave were worshiping the pool or waterfall. It could be possible that they did this during one of their holy days. I've read about tribes that believed in magical powers of waterfalls and pools or lakes. I could totally believe that people accidentally came into this cave and thought that there was some type of supernatural element to it or even magic. Maybe they believed that bathing in the pool or standing under the waterfall would give them fertility or strength or eternal life. Ponce de Leon believed a fountain of youth was real enough to sail across the ocean and that was only five hundred years ago, so it's not that far of a stretch.

There are scatterings of handprints along the way in no observable pattern. They are various sizes in black, red and off white. I study the sizes of the hand and determine that there were dozens of different hands, and

they are all left hands. The paintings depicted two people and two goats. I wonder why the other two aren't
depicted in the mural. There could have been more
than one trip to the cave or they even could have been
women or children which would not have been fea-
tured in art of this time period. Whether it was two or
four people or even more is not too relevant, but it is
encouraging because it shows that the cave is capable
of supporting multiple people over an extended period
of time. My miracle this morning is a prime example
of this. These people could have been early Christians
too. It is fun to imagine early Christians where I am
right now, thanking him for his provision. I bet they did
a better job of trusting God for their daily needs than I
do.

I'm out of light for the cave paintings so I go over to
my lists and update my tally marks for how long I've
been here. It's been six days. Would the person I was
in my cubicle at work recognize who I am now? I think
back to the twenty-eight hash marks on the painting.
Like a hidden-picture game, once I see I can't unsee it.
The marks were a way of keeping track of time for people who painted it and those coming after. The long
and the short of it is that twenty-eight days is a long
time trapped in a cave. But it's also a finite amount of
time as opposed to forever or someday. It's easier to believe in the supernatural here without all of our science
and technology, so against all logic I'm going to believe

that I will be rescued or escape on the twenty-eighth day.

Kevin

Today feels like when you're on your last day of vacation: still hopeful, but that hope is diluted by the impending end of the trip and all the stress that is waiting for you back home. I wake up feeling exactly like that. Think positive, I tell myself. Nothing good is achieved by negativity. I had a professor who frequently told me, "Positivity produces productivity, but negativity incubates failure." I take a moment to ask God for guidance and to help me trust Him completely.

When I emerge from my tent, the men have already eaten and are sitting around the fire. Pelo nods and motions for me to join them. They have one of the chewy protein-rich rice bars that his wife made laid out for me with some water. I snatch it up and try to catch up with their conversation. Nakul is arguing with Pelo, "Just because we don't see tracks doesn't mean she didn't walk away from the rock."

Ibrahim joins in, "As I've been arguing, we can't discount there being a predator. I agree with Nakul, the absence of tracks does not mean that nothing else happened."

Pelo raises his hands. "Ok, ok. You've made your point. I have been trying to be logical about this, but that has left us empty-handed. I agree that we need to search and explore any possible scenario." He spreads his arms wide. "I'm all ears."

There is a jumble of conversations happening simultaneously attempting to explain her disappearance. Some theories are more believable than others. A stealthy predator like a mountain lion? Maybe. An aerial attack from a vicious condor? That's a stretch. A lovesick yeti? Inconceivable! I'm a scientist, and that one is hard to swallow.

These wild scenarios have left me baffled and, frankly, scared. I clear my throat and try to bring the discussion back on topic. "I think what we can take away from all of these scenarios is that we need to expand our search. We can have some guys search for places a bear or mountain lion or large bird," at this I massage my temples, "could have carried Charlotte off to. Others will search around the mountain for places that Charlotte could've hiked to if she was disoriented. As we say back home, 'No stone left unturned.'"

Each of them nods in agreement and we discuss groups. Nakul and Ram are the best hunters and trackers and are selected to search for lairs that a predator could have carried her off to. The remaining ones split up between hiking up the mountain and exploring the immediate area more thoroughly. We each take more protein bars and water with the explicit instruction to meet back at camp by sundown, no exceptions. Pelo keeps me in his group again, and we are assigned to searching east of the clearing.

This stage of the search is much different than the hike up. Our trip up the mountain was primarily focused on getting up here quickly but safely. I start out climbing up the rocks and boulders that make the eastern cliff face of the clearing. At the top we pause for a breather. Pelo points out a game trail on the side of the mountain, likely from mountain goats. Pelo tells me, "We can take this trail but will have to go down single file. The trail will be rough, so don't be afraid to take it slow. If you ever feel like you're going to fall, just sit. We only have a few hours left to search because it will take longer to hike back up."

I nod in acknowledgement. "My motivation for this hike is pretty low. I actually don't see the point in searching over here. The bush she walked over to is on the opposite side of the clearing."

Pelo places both hands on my shoulder and says, "Look at me." I look up and sigh. "If, and I only mean if, we went down the mountain having not found Charlotte, could you live with yourself if you had not searched every possible place she could have gone? Even the unlikely ones?"

I sigh. "No, I guess not. I just want to be the one to find her, you know? Her knight in shining armor showing up to save the princess."

"Even if one of the others finds her, you will still be her knight because you're here. You didn't give up on her," Pelo explains.

"Yeah, I guess so. Ok," I let out a deep breath, "Let's go, Billy."

"Who's Billy?" I ask, looking around in confusion.

"You are. Get moving, Billy Goat," he replies with a quiet "baaaaa." I'm too depressed to laugh, so I don't. I just roll my eyes and follow.

We hike down the eastern side of the mountain, constantly on the lookout for any signs someone came this way. After about two hours of hiking, the trail connects with the main hiking trail up the mountain. When I see this I collapse to my knees, upset at our failure. Pelo pats my back and tells me to take a break. I jerk away and yell, "I don't want a break. I don't want another stupid protein bar. I just want Charlotte!" My vision is going dark, and I feel like I'm going to pass out.

Pelo helps me sit. "Ok, just breathe. In and out. Sit down and put your head between your knees. Slow breaths."

I do as he says. As I slow down my breathing, my vision returns and the roaring in my ears quiets.

Pelo kneels next to me. "Ok, I understand you're upset, but we can't be yelling out here, alerting every predator around that there are two tasty snacks on the trail. Take a second to catch your breath and let's head back up and see what the others found."

I am dejected and depressed. My positivity has evaporated like the fizz from a soda, and I'm left with a flat Diet Coke. The hike up the game trail is grueling, and I'm dragging my feet all the way. My attitude could give the Grinch a run for his money. When we climb over the last rock into the clearing, I jog over to the campsite hoping that just maybe one of the others found her. Everyone else is back sitting around the fire, resting up from their hikes, but there are only four people, and none of them is Charlotte. I don't say anything to anyone. I just walk over to my tent, crawl in and zip it closed. This day just needs to end.

Chapter 9

Day 7

"*When you come to the end of your rope, tie a knot and hang on.*"
Franklin D. Roosevelt

My body wakes again on its own, and I feel refreshed and rested. The human body has a built-in circadian rhythm and will naturally get tired based on the sun, but it can be influenced by light, exercise and stress. It is a twenty-four-hour internal clock that regulates our sleep, metabolism and hormones. I used to tell people I was a morning person, but that was not completely true. I was a morning person by necessity, not because I actually enjoyed it or naturally woke up early. My college years and my career required me to rise early for a long commute or to get to the office early and get things done before everyone else arrived. Just because I was up early does not mean I was rested or getting enough sleep. In fact, I have probably spent over half of my life sleep-deprived. I frequently have said, "Who needs sleep? I'll sleep plenty when I'm dead."

The doctors all prescribe a full night's sleep as part of the treatment for anxiety and depression. I have met some people in life who really did wake up early and were a literal ray of sunshine. When I was young I had a friend whose dad would wake up early and go around the house singing, quite loudly, she complained, "Rise and shine and give God the glory glory." So waking up with a positive attitude is a foreign concept to me.

I begin my day as I have the previous with thanking God for all the good things in my life. Then I stretch and head to the pool for water. I am nervous to look at the greens and wild onions and mushrooms. Maybe yesterday was a bizarre accident, and I realize that this is doubt, so I push that out of my mind and trust that God's miracle has continued today. And it has. Yesterday was overwhelming and shocking to see how God provided for me. However, his continued provision is even more of a blessing, and I cry and thank him for that. I get a big drink from the pool and a light breakfast. My brain is boggled that what I have been eating the last few days has sustained me because the math of the nutrition just doesn't add up. On paper greens, tubers, and mushrooms aren't enough calories and protein for a complete day's diet. This is just another example of God's provision in my life. He's not only providing for the quantity of what I need to eat but also the quality. I think about what Jesus taught the disciples who were worried about the future and material things like what they would eat, drink and wear. He told them, "The father already knows what you need before you even ask." He has provided more than enough; in fact, he also provides for us even better than what we expected. It might not be what we were asking for, but it will be good and exactly what we need.

With my belly full and rested, I ask God quickly to guide and direct my day and to give me wisdom. I follow the light and head back to the cave paintings. I decide to look at them from a distance and close up. I back up and "zoom out" so I can take in the whole of the mural at once. Some sections are random, whereas the center part with the animals and pool seems to be painted more with more detail and care. I'm no expert in art or history, but the central scene of the painting appears the most detailed but also the oldest. The lines of the drawings are bolder, while the colors of the hands and other random drawings around are brighter, which I can only assume could mean the pigments of the materials used have faded more from age.

I "zoom in" and start to examine the handprints around the central painting. I hold my hand up to one handprint and compare the size. This one does not only have longer fingers but also wider ones than mine. I try other handprints and find them to be various sizes, but all were the same as mine or larger. I think it's safe to say that these handprints all came from adults, and mostly from people my size or larger. This is not hard considering that I am a small woman, only five foot two inches. The handprints are not in any observable pattern, color-wise or spacing-wise or even direction. They are random, but there are some groupings but not large ones. There are sets of two or three that are a little closer together but not identical. I'm starting to have several theories about the handprints. First, they are not all made by the same two or three people. Second, they are not all made at the same time. Finally, the handprints are not made out of desperation but celebration or even a way of marking a big achievement, much like how someone would leave their initials at the top of a large water tower or after climbing a cliff. This is a very remote region of the world, and I have no knowledge of their indigenous peoples. I am tempted to compare them culturally to the indigenous peoples of America and see what, if any, similarities there could be.

For example, what if the people who drew these paintings originally found this cave by accident, like I did? Maybe they returned to their village and told the story of finding this remarkable place full of what would be considered at that time supernatural phenomena and possibly natural resources. People could have returned to find the cave on purpose. They might have found an entrance that has since collapsed. Maybe they dug into the mountain until they found it. If I pursue the mythical line of logic about a regular occurrence of an opening into the cave every twenty-eight days, they could have attached a spiritual meaning to it. Some primitive tribes worshiped gods or spirits of the earth and sky or ones that resided in holy places.

The enormity of this connection hits me, and I have to move to the center of the cave with the light to my lists. I begin to add to them what I have theorized this morning. Logically these theories seem far-fetched: however, if someone had told me a month ago that I would fall into a cave while hiking in the mountains with all these miraculous things happening, I would have laughed at them and said that sounds like a good idea for a novel.

I take a break for lunch and then follow the light to the far end of the cave, where I can still occasionally hear the wind blow through the cracks. I lean back against a large stalagmite and examine the cave wall with cracks in different sizes going various directions. The wall is large and is hard to take in at once. I've seen archaeologists start a dig by gridding it off. I find a piece of granite with a sharp edge and grid off all the areas I can reach in a three-by-three hand-with section by scraping the sharp edge of the rock on the wall. This is very difficult, and my forearms are burning from how much pressure it takes to barely leaving faint, nearly invisible lines. This type of marking on the wall is not ideal, but I feel it might provide some useful data. If I pursue the theory that an opening will appear in a twenty-eight-day cycle, it could be possible that one of these cracks could get large enough for a person to go through. I need a baseline for the size so I can measure the cracks to see if any are expanding or even contracting. I measure each crack by the width of my thumb, approximately one inch, and record it in the grid. I have to work quickly before I lose the light and finish in just enough time to make it back to the pool for an evening meal and drink. I collapse into my bed of moss with my mind whirling from today's discoveries.

Kevin

Sleep is a blessed relief from the pain, but I wake up feeling just as depressed as when I collapsed in the tent and fell asleep yesterday. Somehow I have to hike miles down the mountain, again, leaving my wife behind, and this time maybe permanently. I'm angry and not good company to be around. When someone tries to talk to me, I just ignore them or glare at them until they shut up. After packing up, we begin hiking in near silence. We make it past the hardest part of the descent, and everyone has tried to console me.

Ibrahim hikes beside me and says, "Hey, Kev, you gotta talk this out. I know how you're feeling. I lost my wife to breast cancer a year ago. If you keep this bottled up inside you're going to self-detonate."

I snap at him. "Don't tell me you know how I'm feeling! None of you know! Having someone die is not the same as them just disappearing into thin air. The only thing that could even slightly compare would be kidnapping, but even then you could investigate it and maybe even get your loved one back. I don't get that opportunity. Charlotte disappeared and that's it. She's gone. Dead, I presume now. So back off. I don't want your sympathy and empty platitudes."

My words are dripping with hatred and venom. What I just screamed at them is the tame version of what I want to say, but I'm trying to rein it in because of all they've done for me. My sanity is hanging on by a spider's web thread, and it would only take a feather right now to send me on a one-way trip to the funny farm or jail.

There's silence, and I know I've hurt them. I sigh and adjust my pack. "Just keep walking. It's not you guys' fault. I know you're just trying to help, and I really do appreciate it. I'm just angry." I rub my eyes with the backs of my hands, forcing the tears back where they belong, "and scared," I whisper. They all nod. "Let's just get down this cursed mountain."

We make a two-day hike in just one, and I'm back in my bed at the lodge by dark. I get in bed not even bothering to change my clothes, bathe or eat. I just curl up with Charlotte's pillow, breathing in her scent as I fall asleep from sheer exhaustion. Prayer is the furthest thing from my mind. It's hard to tell what I'd say to God right now.

Chapter 10

Day 8

"Survival can be summed up in three words - never give up. That's the heart of it really. Just keep trying."
Bear Grylls

My body knows it's morning, but I just lie on my pallet for a moment thinking about my research on the cracks in the cave wall. I measured them but didn't have time to process or analyze what they could represent. The limited light is a major restriction for trying to work anywhere. I feel like I'm making some progress and then must stop and move on. Another restriction is not having the ability to write things down. I can write on the floor, but it's difficult because I have to print and the writing is large due to writing with my finger. My lists and notes take up a lot of valuable surface area that I have to walk around. Also, the surface is not smooth, so the words aren't always legible. The same would be true for painting on the cave walls. I doubt the people who painted this cave had written language, but if they did I would understand why they didn't use it. Pictures and symbols would be much easier to draw and to read.

After my morning routine of stretching and thanking God for his blessings in my life, I go to the pool and eat my breakfast. I am not smelling the greatest, so I plan at lunch today to figure out how to bathe and if it's possible to clean my clothes.

I head over to the paintings and decide to study them up close today. I cannot draw a grid on these paintings like I did on the other wall, but I mentally apply one based on the "sections" of the painting. First, I realize that there are only two handprints on the right. Most ancient languages read from right to left, so I am going to stick with that. I examine the handprints, and it is obvious that they are not the same two hands. They are larger than my hand, but I do not think that they are the hands of an adult male. My imagination is running wild, and it is hard for me to think clearly without having fantastical imaginations. It's important to remember that I am trapped in this cave, so it could be possible that I am losing my mind. However, it is widely accepted that the world as we know it is much larger than we think. Modern science and logic, historically speaking, are new concepts. Before the industrial revolution, most things that were not known or could not be explained were attributed to a supernatural force or witchcraft.

NASA even admits that most of the universe is unknown. They estimate we only know five percent of it.
The other ninety-five percent is stuff we cannot see
or understand. This cave, even though not in space, is
definitely in that ninety-five percent. Like outer space,
much of prehistoric human development is speculation
and inference.

I am going to attempt to put my headspace into the
thought process of a young person who has either accidentally or purposely come into this cave. As one of
the early visitors to the cave, I think one of the first
things I would want to do is mark that I had been
there, much like planting a flag on the moon. Drawing
my handprint on the cave wall would be the equivalent
of writing "John wuz here 1991" in your new school
locker. It would be there for everyone else who uses it
afterwards to see that you were there first.

The handprints are painted at a height that is within
my reaching distance with my arm stretched straight
forward. I am assuming that these individuals were the
same height as me. This makes sense because I have
heard research that the modern average human has become gradually taller over the last millennia. Even a
shorter-than-average modern female would be approximately the same height as a fully grown adult male
caveman. Kevin has given college lectures on this topic,
including a funny anecdote about how his petite wife
would be as tall as an adult male caveman, accompa-

nied by a wedding picture of me standing over a foot shorter than his six-foot-tall frame.

I have no way of knowing how far back these paintings date, if it's a few hundred years or even thousands of years. Carbon dating would be able to determine the age, but there's no other way to know. Part of me thinks that it would be more recent because of how vibrant the colors are, but without weather and erosion in the cave, they would last longer than ones exposed to the elements.

There's not much more I can study in this section, so I head back to the pool to address my hygiene, or lack thereof. I drank water from the pool but have not tried to enter it, other than accidentally when I fell. The edges of the pool are clear and the water is calm, except for ripples from the stream's waterfall. The grasses and moss that surround it make for a verdant fringe, albeit a slippery one.

I know from drinking the water that it is the temperature of the cave, probably around sixty degrees. Getting in the water is a risk because of the temperature and not having a way to dry off or get warm. This has to happen because my scalp is itchy, and I am grimy from the rocks and dust of the cave. I know I have to wash my clothes, so I strip down near the edge of the pool on some moss. Leaning over the edge, I dunk my shirt and pants and undergarments in the water, scrubbing them together like I've seen women do by the riverside in documentaries on TV. At least I don't have to watch out for crocodiles and pythons. I take a rock and use it to scrub some stubborn stains and areas where the odor is the worst. I rinse again and repeat until they look better and smell fresher.

Now that they are clean, I have to figure out how to dry them. I'm going to have to go about in the nude while they do so. I come up with the idea of draping them over stalagmites with the point going through the neck hole of my shirt and waist of my pants. I spread my button-up flannel over two stalagmites. My shirt fabric is thinner, so hopefully I can get it dry before bedtime, but my heavy hiking pants may not be dry till the next day. This means that washing them will not be able to be a frequent thing due to drying time, but the cooler temperature means that I'm not sweating like I would in the outside world, I realize.

My new organic, gluten-free diet is making my skin less oily. I go back to the pool and think about how I need to wash myself. I don't want to completely submerge in the water because I fear hypothermia. I decide to sit on some moss on the side of the pool and stick my feet in. I cup my hands for some water to wash. I see a rock with a cup–like shape to it. It only holds maybe two cups of water, but at least it's not dribbling out of my hands. I pour water over my arms, legs and torso, rubbing off the dirt, then rinse. Then, just like washing a baby's hair, I rinse my hair, scrub my scalp with my fingers then rinse my scalp again. I don't get my hair overly wet. It is matted enough for me to braid and stay together without a hair tie. This is a novelty for me because normally my hair is so silky that it won't stay styled like this without an excessive amount of hairspray.

I feel very self-conscious in the nude, but I have to remind myself that there's no one to see me and this is a necessary activity. I eat my lunch and rest in the moss, which is warm, waiting for the light before I head to the other side of the cave.

The light has traveled to the far side of the cave, and I go over there to study the cracks again. I look at my data from yesterday, and I'm not sure how it is supposed to help me. I lean back against a large rock, still in the nude, and I feel frustrated. While I was studying it, I felt hopeful that there would be something that would give me information. But I don't see a pattern in any of the cracks, and I don't see how studying this will help me. I am exhausted from doing laundry and bathing, so I go to check on my clothes. My undergarments are dry and I put them on with great relief. My shirt is mostly dry, and I put it on knowing that my body heat will dry it the rest of the way quickly. My pants, however, are not going to be done until tomorrow.

Kevin

Today was supposed to be our last day at the lodge; a day for us to pack and rest from the strenuous hike.

Instead, I am packing my stuff and hers by myself. Alone. As much as I would love to stay in case she were to show up, I know that I have to be on that plane this evening to connect to tomorrow's flight or be stuck here for days. These flights are expensive, difficult to arrange, and non-refundable. I have to take the flight from here back to Lukla, another mountain village that has a tiny airstrip providing regular turboprop flights back to Kathmandu. I'll fly there and stay the night before the flight heads to Munich and finally to Pittsburgh. It will be a very long, lonely trip home. It's almost twenty-four hours with layovers. I left her driver's license, passport and some money at the lodge for Charlotte in case she were to show up later. She would need them to be able to get home. Finally, I snapped a picture on my phone of her documents so that I had all of her personal information with me. I'm hoping she will make it home on her own, but I am mentally preparing for the worst.

After packing, I set our bags by the front door and go to the dining room. It has large windows to take in the mountain vistas. Sitting at a table I prop my feet up on the chair across from me. Every muscle hurts and my feet have blisters and sores. Sita sees me and comes over to ask if I'm hungry, but just the thought of food makes me sick. Anxiety and anger are churning my stomach into rancid butter.

"Vodka," I tell her. "And bring the bottle. No glass."

"I'm sorry, Mr. Kevin, but we don't have any alcohol. Besides, it wouldn't help your problems anyways," she replies.

"Oh, it would fix one big problem right now." I tap my temple with my finger. "I need to forget. I need to escape. I need to numb the pain." I turn away from her before I say more. I feel like I am going to puke up my pain and rage. I would hate for her to be the recipient of that. Sita just shakes her head sadly and walks away, leaving me to stare angrily out the window.

She returns just minutes later with a cup of steaming tea.

"What am I supposed to do with that?" I ask with a snort.

"Drink it. Slowly. Look out at the mountains and quiet your mind. There's not very much a good cup of tea can't fix." She leaves me alone with the tea and my thoughts. I haven't had hot tea since I was sick at my grandma's when I was seven. I tentatively sniff the cup, and the steam fills my sinuses with the aroma of strong black tea and lemon and honey. Holding the hot cup in my hand, I look at the window and blow a puff of air across the tea, then breathe in the steam. The first sip is like drinking a memory. I stare out the window, just blankly, breathing deeply and sipping tea. By the time I have drained my cup, I'm relaxed enough to go back to my room and sleep.

Chapter 11

Day 9

" These scars tell the story, but they don't define you."
Jelly Roll

I fell asleep chilly. I wake up cold. Not winter-in-Pittsburgh cold, but still, cold. My pants will hopefully be dry by afternoon. I made sure to place them near the center of the cave so that they would get the mid-day sun that's warmer. I'm struggling with my gratitude list today. It's hard to be thankful when situations have made your life miserable. My life above ground looked good on paper. Everyone wanted to be me. I had it all then lost it all only to realize that what I had wasn't worth having. I had a great husband, successful career, and money. Everyone wanted to be me. Except me. I was miserable, depressed, anxious and trapped in the pursuit of my career. Now my internal conflicts have transformed from feeling internally trapped to external entrapment in this cave.

Yeah, I'm alive, but I'm cold and stuck in a cave. I ask God to help me rejoice in my trials. This was one of my least favorite verses to hear preached. I don't want to rejoice. I want to complain and throw a fit about how life isn't fair. My faith is being tested, and right now it's barely passing. I have an ember left, but I need it to grow into a flame.

I pray, "God increase my faith. I do trust you but help me trust you more. You haven't failed me yet. I am miraculously alive in this cave. I have to believe that you have a purpose for me in all of this. I look forward to see how you will turn this test into my testimony. Help me, Lord."

I cry in frustration, but my stomach is grumbling, so I have to get up and move. Smaller meals with less calories necessitate that I eat more frequently. I feel like today is not going to be very productive. But if I survive the day and get my pants dry, I'll take it as a win.

I'm not good at being miserable. Usually I can only stay mad for an hour before I'm tired of being mad. It makes me literally feel bad. My face gets flushed, and my blood pressure spikes. I perk up a little after eating. I don't know how God provides all my nutritional needs through these plants, but I feel better than ever. I make a vow that I doubt I'll be able to keep to eat healthy and organic after I escape. I read somewhere that unhealthy eating can influence your mental health. I fully believe it because after I started eating the food here I could feel a change in my attitude and emotions. What other reason could there be for me not being insane after eight days trapped in a cave! Who knew grass could do that?

I check my pants after lunch, and thankfully they're dry enough to wear. Thank the Lord. I would never survive in a nudist colony. I've wasted the whole morning waiting on my pants, so I determine to be productive this afternoon. I head to the far end of the cave to check on the cracks. Based on my grid that is barely visible, there appears to be no change in any of the cracks. I have wondered if it would be possible to expand the cracks by chiseling through with sharp rocks, but, as I discovered with trying to mark lines, this is near impossible without tools or sustainable to work at for an extended period of time. I imagine the width of the cave wall to the outside is several feet thick or more. I feel defeated because I have basically eliminated one of my potential escape plans.

Kevin

The flights home were grueling both physically and emotionally. On every flight there was an empty seat next to me, a constant reminder that I left someone behind. I finally land in the States after midnight and take an Uber back to our apartment. It doesn't feel like home without her. I drop my bags at the front door and throw myself on the couch. It was so difficult to keep the emotions reined in while traveling. I haven't let myself cry until now. But here at home I let it all out. Crying, screaming, beating the couch with my fists. I throw the fancy pillows on the couch across the room, knocking over a lamp with a crash. I cry until my head hurts worse than my pain. My shirt is soaked with my tears, and I use it to wipe my face. Crying has helped me release some of the bottled-up fear, pain and rage. Then comes being numb like a zombie. There's a point with pain that your brain can't take any more, so it shuts down your feelings and you become numb to the pain.

International flights always land late and it's now after two a.m. My suitcase and bags are still by the front door, and I couldn't care less. The drain of the travel catches up with me, and I pass out from exhaustion on the couch still fully clothed.

Chapter 12

Day 10

"In three words I can sum up everything I've learned about life: it goes on."
Robert Frost

Yesterday was a wash. I woke up this morning feeling like I had wasted valuable time. What if I am close to finding a way out and instead of searching yesterday I laid around feeling sorry for myself just because my pants were wet? Every moment wasted here is another minute I'm separated from Kevin and my family and freedom. I vow to renew my efforts and attitude to finding a way out. To quit searching would be to give up hope of escape or rescue. Hope is the only thing keeping me alive. Giving up is the first step of dying. At any moment I could admit defeat and just accept that this is it. Resisting the temptation to quit is a constant struggle. Quitting is always easier than pressing forward. Perseverance requires hope and sometimes hope hurts. The Bible says, "Hope deferred makes the heart sick but its desire fulfilled is a tree of life." Trees produce fruit and the fruit of our hope-tree is faith. How long do I want to be hope-sick? My hope to see Kevin and the sun again is stronger than my despair.

It's so quiet in the cave. My breathing is the loudest sound other than the quiet roar of the waterfall and wind whistling. I initially was scared to make noise because of movies that I have seen with caves collapsing due to loud sounds. This cave is large and stable enough that it would take a supersonic volume to trigger that kind of damage.

To drown out the deafening silence I talk to myself like how Tom Hanks talked to "Wilson" while stranded on the island in the movie *Castaway*. It's a shame that I don't have a volleyball down here to keep me company like he did. I have talked to myself my whole life, but being here alone it has increased tenfold. Normally I needed to have music or audiobooks or the TV on in my life because I didn't like the silence and how it made me feel alone and my thoughts exposed. Reciting scripture that I have memorized has been a big comfort. I know there are many verses that I am paraphrasing and I'm sure there are certain people that would offend. Personally, I don't think God speaks King James and since I don't have a Bible here I have to do the best I can. I have been surprised and pleased at how much I remember. I am thankful for the times I have spent in my younger years reading my Bible. It has been my lifeline while trapped here.

Besides talking, I've been singing too, mostly worship and hymns. When a song comes to mind, I just start singing and keep on at it until I have it out of my system. I have sung in the church praise band since I was sixteen and played piano and guitar and drums over the course of my life. When my career got busy I stopped going to church because I said I didn't have time. I miss worship at church, feeling connected to everyone there, encouraged by the words, and feeling his spirit fill me. With no one around, I can sing as loud or as goofy as I want. Singing brings me joy. It was hard to sing the first time in here, because I didn't feel like being thankful, happy or joyful. The first song I sang was "It Is Well with My Soul." I cried and my singing did not sound good because I was snotty and congested, but peace filled me and the more I sang the better I felt. Singing praise is waging war against the devil. I remember the story about the battle where God told the king to send the singers out first. We thank God and sing his praises before the battle because we can't see from our viewpoint that he has already fought it and won. Praise makes future victories present realities.

This morning a scripture came to me that was a great comfort. I heard it preached at a Palm Sunday service once. After Jesus came into Jerusalem, and everyone was shouting "Hosanna!" and waving their palm branches, the Pharisees were angry and told Jesus to tell the crowds to be quiet. Then Jesus told them that if his disciples stopped that the rocks would cry out his praise instead. Looking around at all the rock in my cave, it's staggering to think about how much praise that would be, if all the rocks exploded in praise. I sit and place both of my hands on the rock floor beside me palm down. I'm not a hippie, but I'm imagining the praise that is bottled up inside of this rock. I placed my hands over my chest and I do the same thing. I am created in God's image and I am filled with his praise. I start to sing a song without words, it is very melodic, in a minor key, and it comes from somewhere deep in me. It's just notes, but they're coming from my soul and because I know God knows my heart he knows and receives my praise. My day wasn't physically productive, but a lot of work got done in my heart. After searching the cave all day and praising Him with every breath, I end my day thanking God until I fall asleep.

Kevin

When I wake up, the first thing I feel is dry mouth and fuzzy teeth. I can't stand my mouth feeling fuzzy. Then the call of nature wakes up too. I take care of those things, and immediately a headache and jet lag double-team me, and I wobble on my feet from vertigo. Once the room comes back into focus, I splash water on my face from the bathroom sink then look up in the mirror. I don't recognize the man in it: ashen skin, sunken lifeless eyes with dark circles and a scraggly beard. I don't have the energy to shave, but I desperately need coffee and aspirin. My head is pounding while I make the coffee and decide what I need to tackle today.

I grab a notepad from the bar and sit down with my coffee at the breakfast table. Our apartment has a stunning view of the Allegheny River. Charlotte picked this apartment for that reason solely. She had a busy career and used lists and sticky notes to keep herself organized. There were notes left for me frequently, too, mostly chores not to forget. She was the one who liked making lists and I take a play out of her book now and start with a "To-Do" list.

The first bullet is to call her mom and dad. This will be a bloodbath because they will blame me, and they have every right to. She disappeared while on vacation with me. They both have high-profile careers and both thought, even though they never said it out loud, that she married below herself. They won't want any negative press coming from this that would reflect poorly on their careers or hers.

Next, I need to go to the police. I'm not sure how to proceed, and I need someone to guide me. Maybe I was supposed to do something in Nepal. I don't know; I feel guilty, scared and very alone.

Another bullet point is to get another trip planned to go back and continue searching for Charlotte. I owe it to her to try again. I will have to take time off work, maybe even a sabbatical, get funds ready for tickets and gear and maybe hire some professionals to help investigate. This step gives me something concrete to do and a glimmer of hope. I can't give up.

The last bullet point is blank. I'm thinking about who I can call to support me. My father died the summer after high school, and my mom passed before I finished my PhD. I was out of the country on a dig when she had a massive stroke. She died alone, and I will never forgive myself for that. I would give anything to be able to talk to them now and ask them what to do, or feel mom scratch my back. "Why, God?" I mentally ask. "It's too much." I briefly consider calling my pastor, but we haven't been in church since Christmas, so that would be awkward.

I've never felt this alone in my life. Dark thoughts about self-harm circle my head like vultures. Giving up is the easy way out. Romeo's dilemma makes sense; there's no life without her. However, I'm stubborn and determined, and I'm not dead yet. I have a mission, and that's enough to keep me above ground for now.

The phone call to Charlotte's parents requires another cup of coffee. It's been days since I've eaten; I know I need to eat, but I don't think I could keep it down right now. Plus there's no food in the apartment right now. Calling her father makes more sense because he has a desk job while her mother is frequently in court as the DA. They divorced shortly after Charlotte was born. It was one of the few marriages where you see the couple and think, "Yeah, I get it. Those two are not good for each other." But they did a good job co-parenting Charlotte, mostly, but no one's perfect. I scroll through the contacts on my phone and select Charlotte's father's name, Charles Vandonberg, retired Army Ranger, then state representative, and now in his retirement, a "consultant" at the Pentagon, whatever that means. He'll probably keep working until his heart gives out. I tap his name on my screen. The phone rings once then a woman answers, "Mr. Vandonberg's office, how can I help you?"

"Yes, good morning. This is Kevin, his son-in-law. I need to speak with him as soon as possible. I'm afraid it's a family emergency," I tell her with some conviction, knowing that if I want to get through to him I'll need to be theatrical.

"Of course, right away, Kevin. Let me transfer you back to him now."

The line beeps three times, then a gruff voice that has given me many nightmares answers. "This is Vandonberg."

"Mr. Vandonberg. This is Kevin, your son-in-law." I pause for acknowledgment but there's none. "Sorry to bother you this morning, but I have some disturbing news," I stammer.

"Did Charlotte lose all that money she invested in Yakima stock?" He yells.

I sigh. "If only." I clear my throat and cut to the chase. "When Charlotte and I were hiking Mt. Pheriche, there was an accident."

"Oh, God. She broke a leg, right? She's always been so clumsy. Those gymnastics lessons were a waste of money and time. God, if she wasn't already crippled, I'd beat her," he grumbles.

"Um, no, that's not it either." I take a deep breath. "We were hiking together and she jumped off a large rock and," I pause, "disappeared," quietly spoken.

"What exactly do you mean by 'disappeared?'" he grinds out slowly.

"We stopped for lunch halfway up the mountain and she walked away to use the bathroom in privacy. I watched her jump off a large rock and vanish," I explain.

There's silence, and I look at my screen to make sure he didn't hang up on me. Nope. "Let me get this straight. She jumped off a rock and, poof, was gone."

"Yes, sir, that's the long and short of it."

"Please explain to me carefully and in great detail what efforts you have made to find my daughter and bring her home," he orders. I relate to him that I searched until dark and hiked down to get help from the locals. I leave out the part about the local superstitions about the mountain.

"Why didn't you go get help from the embassy or police?"

"Sir, the police were hours away, there are no roads, the weather is unpredictable, and the police would have done exactly what the locals did. Then my time ran out and I had to leave in order to be able to make it back to the States at all," I defend myself.

Yelling again, "You lost my daughter, failed to find her, then returned home without her." He's breathing so hard I can feel it on my neck clear from the Pentagon. "You're a sorry excuse for a husband!"

His exclamation confirms my greatest fears: I am a horrible husband and an even worse man. In one phone call I have confirmed all of the doubts he's had about me since Charlotte introduced me to him. "Sir, please, in my defense, I had exhausted all my resources and knew I needed to come home to prepare to go back and search again. I want to go back with a team, and I will not return until she is with me."

"Darn right!" There's a crash, as if something was thrown across the room: a coffee cup, by the sound of it. "If she isn't back here soon we will hold you personally responsible, and you can just plan on spending the rest of your life in a very small cell, and that's if her mother gets to you before me." He's quiet again for several seconds, breathing heavily, and I check my phone again. "Charlotte is an adult, and her actions created this situation. You will have our full backing in whatever way you need it for finding her. But I want to make this clear. You either come back with her or don't come back at all. Capiche?"

"Yes, sir. Those were my intentions. My world doesn't exist without her in it."

"Pretty talk doesn't find her, Kevin. I'm going to make some phone calls to people who will get you connected with the right people to make this happen. Flights, guides, gear and money. Get your stuff in order; you're going back in twenty-four hours," he orders.

"Yes, sir," I reply immediately. I clear my throat. "Just one more thing, sir."

"I already know what you're going to ask. She scares me too." He sighs, and I can imagine him rubbing his forehead. "I'll call Charlotte's mother."

"Thank you, sir. I had no idea what to say, and I know she never approved of me, and I just didn't know what to say," I stutter and sniff, trying not to cry.

He interrupts me. "Just stop your blabbering and go find my daughter." He hangs up abruptly with the air of someone who is used to getting what he wants done. This phone call took care of three items on my list. He'll make arrangements for my return and contact the authorities in a way that won't create a media scandal. And call her mother for me.

Chapter 13

Day 11

"When I started counting my blessings, my whole life turned around."
Willie Nelson

My day starts with thanking God and eating the food He has provided for me. I've learned to be specific in my thankfulness. I've heard it said many times and even said it myself, "Thanks for everything." This generic thanks leads to the receiver having less appreciation for the things the giver has done. When I take the time to list each of the things I'm thankful for, it changes my attitude. Because the list of things I'm thankful for is longer than the list of problems I'm facing now.

I have determined to redouble my efforts at exploring the cave for an escape. I start with the cave painting. Was this put here to just be a historical record of these people being here or is there more? I sit down and study the drawings again. I have looked at it so much during my time here that it feels like I don't even see it anymore. I need to look at it with "fresh eyes". There could be something I'm missing.

There was a popular detective show on TV from way back. The detective was eccentric, but his odd techniques would help him solve crime when traditional police got stumped. He would do this thing with his hands where he made a picture frame and looked only through that window to study a crime scene. He would move from one spot to another to look for clues that other officers missed. I feel goofy, but there's no one here to see me. I make an L with my left hand and a backwards L with my right hand hold them up and start to study the paintings while looking through only that square. As I've done before, I start with the older section and study it up close and also at a distance through the frame of my hands. I don't notice anything new there.

Next, I go to the center part of it and study that section. This is where I had found the clue about something that happens in a twenty-eight day cycle. I asked myself, what would Kevin be looking for when he studied this? I think he would be looking for any elements that do not match the style or theme of the rest of the painting. Was anything added later? There is a lot of detail in this section, surprisingly, for the materials they were using.

Using my hand frame and standing close to the wall, I examine the details around the waterfall and pool. I'm on the last section when a design catches my attention that I originally thought was the plants growing around the pool. I look at it again then compare it to the other "grasses" around the pool. They are not the same. Upon further examination, they don't really look like the plants I have been eating, but how they are clustered around the pool did look similar. I consider that this is not a case of primitive drawing, but that it could be symbols or even early writing.

This discovery interrupts my work, and I'm sad because I'm thinking about how much Kevin would love to see this and study it. Instead of being home-sick, I'm Kevin-sick. It is suffocating me, threatening to choke my will to survive.

I whisper, "Kevin, where are you? I need you so much." Tears are threatening to spill out, but I want to keep working. I take a deep breath in and out. I will have quite the story for him if I ever, or I should say when, I get to see him again. I silently ask God for help.

Now that I'm working with the assumption that this design is symbols or even writing, I have to work to decode it. How am I going do that? Time will be my enemy. I can't stay over here all day, and I can't take a picture of it with my phone like I would normally do. I can't even write it down on paper to take with me back to the pool. I'm simultaneously excited and frustrated because I made a breakthrough today and now I've lost the light over here to be able to study it. I give it one last look, trying to commit it to memory before I follow my light over to the middle of the cave. I sit down for a rest and lunch and think about what I've discovered.

My brain is spinning and it's giving me a migraine trying to figure this out. I can feel that it's an important clue and I'm so aggravated at my limited resources to work on it. The pressure of tears is building up again and this is even more frustrating. I don't want to cry! God, help me get off this emotional rollercoaster. I need to breathe and trust that God will help me through this like he has everything else.

As thankful as I try to be, I am just so ready to get out of here. It's been eleven days if my hashmarks are correct. I miss everyone so much: Kevin, my parents, the sun and coffee. The last two are people but I miss them something fierce. I can't let my thoughts go there. Thinking like this is a slippery slope and I've worked so hard to stay positive and focused. The scripture comes to me that helped me so much during college, "I have the mind of Christ." I whisper this over and over and thank God for his wisdom. We will figure this out.

By now I'm mentally and emotionally exhausted so I spend the rest of the day doing some stretching and exercises. Pushing my muscles and working up a sweat is a good release for my frustration. Now I can go to bed tonight physically exhausted, and hopefully wake up rested to tackle this puzzle tomorrow.

Kevin

True to his word, Charles had a car come pick me up in almost exactly twenty-four hours. I have a duffel bag and a larger rolling duffel for hiking gear and MREs. The driver had buzzed up to our apartment that the car was waiting for me. I grab my gear and look around, hoping to see this place again, together with her. Yesterday I took care of placing all the bills on autopay from our savings. The last thing I want is for us to come home and have been evicted.

On the sidewalk outside our apartment building is a soldier trying to look casual in civilian clothes. He loads my bags into the trunk of the town car. "Anything else, sir?"

"Please, don't call me "sir". That's my father-in-law. But no, that's all the bags." He raises a brow but I tell him that the gear in the large duffel is the most important part. "This isn't a walk in the park. People train a long time for these hikes and many have been injured or killed during their trip. We knew the risk but human nature always thinks that 'I'll be the one to beat the odds.'"

He pulls out into congested Pittsburgh traffic. "We will meet the others at the airport."

"Others? I didn't realize more were coming."

"Mr. Vandonberg was clear that he wanted the best Rangers with experience in mountain climbing on the job. You will have the best of the best with you. If she's there, we'll find her."

Something about his statement bothers me. I'm freaking out a little, my hands fisted in my lap. "What do you mean, 'if she's there?' Of course she's there! What are you implying?"

He's silent for a minute and I can see his knuckles turn white as he grips the steering wheel. "Your father-in-law is a very logical, sensible man who looks at a problem from all different angles. You are so close to the situation that you can't see some of the details."

I stare at him, "Continue," I reply, actually thinking 'continue carefully.' My temper is being restrained by a rapidly fraying rope.

"There is a scenario that you have not considered." He pauses and clears his throat. "She may not have disappeared as you have assumed." I'm staring at him but he keeps his eyes on the road. "She might have disappeared," he pauses again, "on purpose."

This is the first time in my life that I've been utterly speechless. Do they really think it's even a remote possibility that Charlotte faked her disappearance to get away from me? Why? To start new somewhere else? None of this makes sense. So that's what my father-in-law thinks about me: I'm that horrible of a husband that she would fake disappearing on a hike in the Himalayas to get away from me. I know that everything I do and say will be reported back to Charles so I force down the anger and hurt those thoughts give me. I'm silently brooding, plotting various ways to get back at him. My anger builds up like the fire in a dragon's belly before he toasts his dinner. I know that Jesus said if you were angry at someone then you've already murdered him with your heart. I feel justified in my righteous anger, but it is toxic.

We meet the other two Rangers at customs but instead of going to a terminal they lead us out to the private airstrip. Charles was sending us in his private jet. I climb aboard and get comfortable in a soft leather seat. I'm still jet lagged from the trip home and now I'm going back before I've even returned back to normal. Thank God we are flying out later in the day so I can sleep the first half of the way. We won't have layovers, just stop for fuel in London. We can take this all the way into Kathmandu. I settle in for another long flight. When we land it will be, I don't know, my brain is too jet lagged to do the math right now. I lean my seat back and thankfully let someone else take the reins.

Chapter 14

Day 12

"Faith and fear both demand you believe in something you cannot see. You choose!"
Bob Proctor

I am psyched! Let's do this. My morning routine is quick so I can get over to the cave paintings as soon as the light reaches them. Rushing through my morning routine, I feel hopeful for some progress today. I'm rushing around and daydreaming about solving the riddle in the message and figuring out how to escape.

After finishing up at the pool, I joyfully jump off a rock, again, imaging the roar of the crowd as I nail a perfect landing from the parallel bars. When I land, my foot hits a loose rock, then my left foot doesn't go where it is supposed to. You think I would have learned my lesson up on the mountain to be more careful, but I have always been a little more clumsy than most, which is why I never succeeded at the balance beam. The rock rolls away taking my foot with it. I fall hard on my ankle and do what is first instinct for any-one: I put my hands out to break my fall so that I don't smack my face on the rock floor. The cave floor rises up suddenly to meet me.

For a brief moment time stops. I am paralyzed with fear and shock. A million scenarios are flying through my brain like a slideshow on crack. The thought of get-ting injured down here and the possible complications that could go along with it had not occurred to me until now. Just like in the tunnel, if I don't open my eyes then it's not real; just a bad dream.

Everything hurts. I'm scared to open my eyes and take assessment of my injuries. I keep my eyes closed and send feelers out through my body to check for damage. My hands are stinging, but that's likely from scraping them on the ground. My knees hurt and are also stinging a little, but I think I can bend them both. When I check on my feet and ankles, Houston, we have a problem. My right foot is fine, but my left ankle is very painful when I try to move. It's swelling already, but I can wiggle my toes so I think it is isolated to my ankle.

I'm laying here hurting, and I'm mad. Not depressed. Not homesick. Just furious. This feels like the last straw. I scream. And I keep screaming. And I start yelling. I'm yelling at God, screaming, "Why did you do this to me? I hate you. This isn't fair! I have been trying so hard to do this your way, and it doesn't work. You want me to trust you and this is what happens. I can have a sucky life without you so if this is all you're going to help me, then I don't want your help in my life!"

I can feel the septic venom in my words, and I wonder where this came from. Have I really felt like this all along? Were these angry, hurtful feelings buried somewhere deep that I didn't know about? Then I cry. What my high school girlfriends called an ugly cry. Snot and crocodile tears and heaving and hiccuping and I keep screaming. This is beyond anger, this is rage. Any rock within my reach is thrown again a cave walls, shattering and spraying rock fragment. Somewhere I know that I have to get it out. I scream and curse and yell lying there on that floor until I have no tears left and my voice is horse. The outburst pacifies the storm and I'm left with the quiet of the aftermath of a hurricane. I curl up in the fetal position on the dusty cave floor like when I have panic attacks, trying to feel smaller and safer.

My therapist called it "Peeling back a layer of the onion." Below all of the anger and rage, I'm scared, and I'm alone. I've been scared for days, but I've been trying to hope, to have faith and trust, and believe that there is a way out and that maybe if I can just hold out, someone will rescue me. In this cave it's difficult to judge time, but I know I laid there a long time. However, bodily functions have a way of motivating us to move. My bladder and stomach tell me that I can't just lay here. I'm stiff from the hard rock floor, and I like I've been in a car wreck. I need to get up and go to the pool.

That's my only coherent thought right now. I have to get up and I have to go to the pool.

I can't walk, but I carefully roll to my side and wince as I put my palms back down on the ground and bring my knees up under me. Then I slowly crawl back to the the pool. It's not that far actually, only about eight feet, but it feels like crawling miles across the surface of the moon. I get to the edge of the pool and rinse the dust and small rocks out the cuts and scrapes on my hands. I whimper in pain as the water washes my cuts and scrapes. I am able to cup my right hand a little to get a few drinks of water which helps my stomach, which is nauseous from the pain. I don't have the energy physically or emotionally to do anything else, including go back to my mossy bed. I just curl up into the fetal position and lay here beside the pool and pass out into a deep dreamless sleep.

Kevin

When I woke I was expecting to see Heathrow Airport, but instead we are still in Pittsburgh. Our flight couldn't take off last night due to thunderstorms. We are slated to take off this morning for London where we will refuel before continuing on to Kathmandu. I'm full of nervous energy, my fingers drumming out a rhythm on my armrest. I can't sleep, read, eat or watch a movie. I open my photos app on my phone, search Charlotte, and swipe through my pictures of her and us. A picture of us smearing cake on each other's faces at our wedding grabs my attention, and I make it my lock screen.

My phone's batter is almost dead so I shut it down and plug it in to charge. Staring out the window at the blurred skyline of the city we made a life in is bittersweet. I feel like the little kid in the backseat of the car whining, "Are we there yet?"

"Hold on, Charlotte. I'm coming," I whisper over and over until I drift off to a Benadryl-induced sleep. My dreams are comforting and bizarre simultaneously. There's a dark cave full of stalactites with a sparkling waterfall flowing into an emerald lake. Shadows fill the cave where a person is curled up sleeping by a lake. Semitransparent wings, like a large white dove, cocoon the woman. I'm scared for her, but I know that she is being protected by a supernatural force.

Chapter 15

Day 13

My right shoulder wakes me up. I didn't move all night. After passing out from the pain yesterday I slept straight through the remainder of the day and night. I can see some faint light in the cracks above the pool so I think it's morning. I'm ashamed of sleeping so long but my body just shut down. I guess I needed it. My doctor always prescribes extra sleep when I am sick because that's when our bodies heal the most. He said during sleep the brain releases chemicals that stimulate growth and repair. Sleep is especially essential for maintaining good mental health. That's if you can fall asleep and stay asleep. My brain never shuts down so my sleep issues complicate my depression and anxiety.

Now that I'm awake, my injuries start to talk to me, and they are all competing for attention. The loudest of them is my ankle. I feel too sore to move, but I tentatively reached down and feel around it. My ankle is a swollen to the same size as my calf. I am clueless and overwhelmed about how to treat it without a trip to the emergency room. My knees are tender and scraped, but don't seem to be have any serious damage. My wrists are sore from the jarring of breaking my fall, but surprisingly there are no cuts or scrapes or swelling. My hands are fine. There's just some very faint pink lines where the cuts used to be. I think that I am hallucinating or maybe dreaming, so I blink my eyes and rub the sleep out then examine my hands again. They are undamaged completely healed. I am shocked and confused, but also a little worried about how trustworthy my perceptions are right now. Things like this just don't happen, right?

I roll to my back and just stare up at the faint light, thinking I'm so lost and confused that I don't even have words. Suddenly, I remember the fit that I threw yesterday when I was angry at God after my fall. I am ashamed of the things I screamed at him and accused him of. I'm afraid he will be angry at me for the things I said. I'm scared that I went too far and that those words will have caused him to turn his back on me. There are some things you just can't say. Those words were the meanest and cruelest that I have ever spoken in my entire life and I am mortified. The conviction and pain of this is even greater than the physical pain I have. I know that I cannot survive without God. None of this was his fault, even though I blamed him for it.

I cover my eyes with my arm and weep for the loss of his help and presence. I am absolutely certain now that I will die here. There's no reason for me to get up and try to drink or eat or try to somehow fix my ankle. It's pointless. God surely has removed his help from my life and only death is certain for my future.

But there is this funny thing about humans. It's not in our nature to die. I wanted to give up on life. What's the point? But our body betrays us until the need to move, use the bathroom, eat and drink overpower the determination we had earlier to give up. The human spirit is strong. It is arguably stronger than our mind because the primitive will to survive, somewhere deep inside me, kicked in.

I'm not absolutely certain that God will not hear my prayers because I cursed him, but there is no one else to yell at. I cursed God. In my pain and rage and frustration, I blamed and hated him for these things. I knew then deep down just as I know with one thousand percent certainty now that these things are not his fault. He did not cause me to fall into a cave. He did not cause me to trip and fall yesterday. But I cursed and blamed a loving and helping God for it. I am so ashamed and humbled by my words, though in the deepest part of my being, I knew I didn't actually hate God. I was just angry and hurt and there's no one else here to blame except myself, so like a child throwing a temper tantrum over not getting his or her way, I did just that to God.

In the off-chance that God is listening and he hasn't turned away from me, I repent. "I want to say how sorry I am for those words I screamed at you yesterday. In that moment, I was angry and full of rage, but I didn't really mean them. It was just frustration and hurt and fear. Because I know in the depths of my soul that you are good. You're so good and you deserve better than this. You already know all this because you can see my heart so look into my heart now and see how much I love you and need your forgiveness."

I'm not completely sure my prayer went anywhere outside of the walls of this cave, but I feel better that I repented in the best way that I know how. I probably will die here in the next few days and it will probably be a miserable death. But I want to at least try. Being miserable is miserable. And the hurt of trying most times is worse than the hurt of doing nothing. I can't just lay here and give up.

I do the only thing that feels right but doesn't make sense to my mind. I'm going to do something I have not yet done in this cave. I twist around so that my feet are pointing toward the pool. Then using my hands, I begin to scoot forward and slide down into it. I have this gut feeling that I need to get into the water. I can't explain it, but I just feel it. The water is cool as I knew it would be and the sides of it slippery with algae, and smooth. I slide down easily until I'm sitting in waist deep water.

The water is warmer as I go forward and following the prompting, I go further until I can't touch the bottom; I'm treading water. It feels so good and I wonder why I haven't done it before, except I know it was fear of what was in the pool and of hypothermia. I'm treading water and I suddenly realize that I am kicking with both feet, not just one. My ankle doesn't hurt anymore. I begin to kick faster and rotate and spin around and it's not just my ankle. My knees don't hurt anymore, my back isn't even sore from laying on the ground. I'm completely healed.

Another idea comes to mind and I just go for it. I hold my breath and dive underwater. I open my eyes and the sight, if I wasn't holding my breath, would take my breath away. It's like being in a crystal fish bowl that's made out of diamonds, sapphires and emeralds all reflecting and refracting this multifaceted light, like an underwater kaleidoscope. If I hadn't personally seen it, I wouldn't believe it. When my lungs feel like they are going to burst I come back up to the surface. I'm looking around at the cave and I think about what was under the water and I'm confused about how these two very different environments can coexist in the same place. I know I can't stay in this pool forever, but I can come back. I doggy paddle to the edge and climb out of the pool to sit. I leave my feet in the water and examine my ankles, clicking my heels together like Dorothy. Then it's like it clicked. This was God healing me. I know it for a fact. I am in a holy place. He hasn't left me to die.

A wave of awe and reverence overcome me. I think back to yesterday and compare it to today and I feel so much shame that I could think those things about God when this provision was just a few feet away from me. My brain feels like it's going to explode out of its skull, but there is no denying the miracle that has taken place. I can see it with my eyes. I can feel it in my body and beyond that, is the unexplainable, peace and comfort that has quieted the storm in my soul from the days I have been here. I let out a deep sigh, and the weight that I've been carrying falls off my shoulders leaves me nearly breathless, and so fatigued, but rested at the same time. I knew that God was providing my food and my water and keeping me safe. Now on top of this, he has become my healer. I wish I could share this with my family and the world. It almost feels selfish to be the only person experiencing this. I firmly believe with full conviction that God's provision and healing must mean that he is taking care of me so that I can survive and get out of this cave and share his goodness with others. Why else would he keep me alive? I can be patient. I can trust that he will show me the way out or I will be rescued and during that time I will be provided for and taken care of by a loving and good heavenly Father. The chorus of the song "Healer" by Hillsong that we sang at church bubbles up inside me and I sing it out loudly with thankfulness and praise.

"I believe you're my healer/I believe you are all I need/I believe you're my portion/you're more than enough for me/Jesus, you're all I need."

Sometimes these words are a declaration of God's provision before we get it and other times, like now, it's a song of praise about how he is providing our needs currently. Even more beautiful is recounting the faithfulness of God through our life, giving us hope that he will continue to take care of us no matter what life throws at us.

I don't even try to get any work done in the cave this morning. I just walk around on my healed ankle singing and praising God. Today was a much-needed praise break. Today some giants were slain.

My bedtime prayer is simple and heartfelt. "God you are good and big and I thank you for everything you have done and will do. I hand the reins of my life over to you. My worry won't get me out or help Kevin wherever he is, so I ask for your help in our lives and I thank you for it even before I see it."

Kevin

Yesterday after the weather cleared, we took the private jet to London, where we stopped briefly for fuel. The captain was concerned by a warning light on the dash so he had a local mechanic check it. The heat sensor for the engine went bad and he was going to have it replaced. Now we will have to wait to fly to Kathmandu until tomorrow. Between these two delays I've lost almost an entire day. We get a hotel room by the airport so we can sleep in real beds tonight.

The worry is making me physically sick. I'm going to have ulcers before this is all over. Everyone keeps telling me to eat, but I'm not hungry because my stomach doesn't even know what day or time it is. I get to my room and flop face-down on the mattress and pass out from sheer exhaustion.

"Exactly how do you expect to climb a mountain when you haven't eaten for days?" Rick asks me.

"I'm not carrying him up," Chad says.

"Not it!" Omar and Gunther say simultaneously. They break out into a heated match of rock, paper, scissors with the loser having to carry me when I inevitably pass out.

"Fine," I grumble. "I'll eat." I'm whining like they're asking me to give away my puppy. "But only because I need to stay strong for Charlotte." I take a bite of some crackers and cheese that John sets in front of me. I'm not normally this dramatic, but the stress is making my stomach feel like I have eels swimming laps in it. I jokingly ask, "Which way would you like me to vomit if these crackers come back up?" They all fake gag, and I smile for the first time in days and immediately feel guilty afterwards. How can I be happy when Charlotte is alone and hurting? But I have a job to do and staying strong is essential for it. I eat small bites and sip water until I feel like I could finally walk without fainting.

My snack made me drowsy and I doze off. The team's voices wake me up. I blink and I can feel my dream slipping away. No! It was something important, I can feel it. There was a lake and a tunnel. Squeezing my eyes shut I try to remember, but the harder I try the less I remember. It was definitely underground and dark yet there was something sparkling. I think it's the same dream from yesterday, and I'm hoping that the dreams are a message or will give us clues. The image fades as I try to hold on to them, but it evaporates like smoke slipping through my fingers.

Chapter 16

Day 14

"*In God's hands, nothing you go through gets wasted. Keep persevering, you have a purpose.*"
Steven Furtick

I used to dread waking up in the morning to go to work. I made a lot of money as broker for our financial firm because I was good at figuring out where to invest my client's portfolios. When they made money, I made money. When the economy went down, we both lost money too. But the stress of it was slowly killing me. I frequently had ulcers and panic attacks. I was under enormous pressure to bring in and keep big clients for our firm. I would wine them and dine them to get them to invest with us. My actual salary was average for being a young broker; it was the large commissions for landing accounts with large portfolios that I thought made all the stress and long hours worth it.

I was trying to work my way up in the firm to get away from this, but that was only possible by outworking everyone. Other brokers competed for the same accounts and that made it stressful to be the best. I survived by daydreaming about what Kevin and I would do when I got the bonus. A cruise or maybe an exotic island vacation? Kevin was always trying to get me to do something adventurous like climb a pyramid while my idea of a vacation is a big book on a quiet beach. But too often we were too busy to enjoy the money. He traveled to various conferences and lectured at colleges all over the world. With my long hours and his travel we didn't get to see each other much. A married couple shouldn't have to schedule a dinner with each other. But somehow that was what our lives had become: two people who shared an address. I was home so little that I couldn't tell you who my neighbors were or if a restaurant in our town went out of business. I had a housekeeper and if we were actually both home for dinner, we would just Door Dash. I used to love to cook, but when I was home I just slept, thinking I could make up for all the hours I missed out on. But everyone knows you never really catch up on sleep.

It's odd to wake up without anxiety, fear or dread. I am legitimately excited to see what the day will hold for me. This experience has changed my life. It would be assumed that anyone who went through an experience similar to mine would be affected by it permanently in some form or fashion. This simple life is so foreign to what I am used to. Other than physical appearance, if you stood the person I was a month ago next to who I am now, I don't think you would recognize them. I know that when I escape or am rescued that my life cannot go back to normal. There will be some drastic changes.

The sunlight that comes through the crack in the top of the cave is the clock that dictates my schedule. I always wear an apple watch or a traditional watch, but I lost it somewhere during my fall. I'm sure even if I had it that it would not be running due to the battery running out or from damage. I still catch myself frequently, looking at my wrist, because some habits are impossible to break. I feel naked without it.

My morning routine is very simple. After I wake, I thank God for all of his blessings in my life and pray for his guidance for today. I do some stretches, then go to the pool for breakfast and a drink.

Next, I go over to study the cave paintings. They have held so many clues and now I am going to attempt to decipher the meaning of the symbols. I feel very strongly that they hold some important information, maybe even how to escape from the cave. It seems obvious to me that people have come and gone from this cave many times. I am trying to commit the symbols to memory. They are unlike anything I have seen before, but somewhat vaguely remind me of Egyptian hieroglyphics. I shake my head as I think about how easy it would be in normal life to take a picture with your phone and Google it and maybe email it to someone for analysis. AI could probably translate it faster than

I can think it. But I don't have those luxuries. I can't search online or call an expert; right now I am the expert. I've studied this painting, looked at it up, close far away from the right and left, and through the picture frame of my fingers. I was excited to study them, but now I feel like banging my head off the cave wall. The morning is nearly passed, and with it the light, and I have not made any progress today. I decide that I will not make any more headway when I am frustrated. I stop for the morning and go to the pool for my midday break.

I'm leaning back against a large rock while chewing a leek and I wonder aloud, "If I could only make a copy of this so that I can take it with me to study by the pool." It's so hard to think clearly when you have a clock ticking in the back of your head while doing it. It's like when you have take the math section on the ACT in sixty-minutes, and the proctor has just said go. With every problem you can feel the seconds ticking away on the clock. Of course, there's more questions than can physically be done during that time, much like life. I have worked under lots of stress and thought I was good at it, but now the stress is attached to the pressure of finding the information for an escape. I feel like when I'm "wasting time" I'm delaying my escape.

It's so frustrating! I can't take a picture of it, and I can't make a drawing of it, except, I can draw it, but just not in the traditional way. I need to think creatively. The tools I have to use make it impossible to write or draw small enough to fit on a flat rock. I could draw the whole set of symbols on a rock, but it would end up being too large and heavy for me to carry. Maybe I can draw them each separately on smaller rocks and bring them back to the pool where I have more hours of daylight to work on them.

Now I have a plan. There are five symbols so I need five thin flat rocks to draw on. I probably need them about the size of a dinner plate, and I know just the place to get them. After a little nap, I head over to the far end of the cave. There are more loose rocks and it looks like they are mostly slate. It has a lateral cleavage so that when it breaks or split, you have a flat service. I looked through the rocks for some of the right size. I will have to bust some up, but I do find one that is usable. I take it back to the pool and will start drawing on it tomorrow. I am pleased with making a little progress today and go to bed thankful for making a small step in the right direction.

Kevin

We landed in Kathmandu last night and stayed the night in the closest lodge. Just like my first trip, a prop plane will take us to Sita and Pelo's lodge later today. I'm looking forward to talking to them again. Who knows where I would be without their help?

Banging on my door jolts me awake. Crusty drool is caked under my face as I open my eyes and try to figure out where I am. Drawing a blank. I check my watch and see that it's night but there's sunlight in the room. The banging continues. "Kevin! Come down for breakfast," more banging. "Kevin!"

At the word breakfast I realize my mouth is dry and chalky. My teeth are still fuzzy. Coffee. That would be nice. Lots of it. I don't remember who these people are but they seem to know me. "Just a minute!" I yell back but my voice is pretty hoarse. Sitting up gives me a little more clarity and the last seventy-two hours comes back to me. The enormity and intensity of everything hits my chest like a Mac truck. It's hard to breathe and I'm shaking and frozen at the same time.

I guess the guys outside were tired of waiting and barged in. They see me sitting on the edge of the bed with my face in my hands, silently shaking. This wasn't what they were expecting to see. A man rushes over to my bed.

"Kevin, hey man, Kev. You ok?" he asks. I can see shoes but can't move. One of them puts a hand on my shoulder, "Dude, you ok?" I still can't reply. It's getting harder to breathe, and my chest is getting tighter. Seemingly from a distance, one man says to the other, "Go get doc and have him come check Kev out." The other man leaves and the one who spoke kneels down beside the bed. He lays the back of his hand against my forehead then on my back. "Kevin, if you can hear me tap your left foot twice." After a second, I tap my foot twice. "Ok, good, good." He pauses, "Just letting you know we're here for you and we'll get this all sorted out."

This sets me off. I sit up and glare at him, "You think you're going to waltz in and sort everything out?" I shout. "I wish you could! But I know better. She's dead and now we're going to traipse around these mountains for days for the long shot chance that we might find her. God! I want to find her so bad. So bad." I run my hands through my hair and pull hard and groan. "God, this is all my fault and I just, I just can't. There's nothing left in me."

The man is silent and I'm still glaring at him. "So do you still want to tell me that we'll get this all 'sorted out'?" I'm provoking him, but honestly I'm up for a fight. It would feel good to let this rage out.

He puffs out his chest and crosses his arms, making his already large frame look larger. Maybe I should pick a fight with a smaller guy. He's six-four at least and probably pushing two hundred fifty pounds, all muscle. He's staring me down like he's sizing me up for a fight. Then he nods and steps toward me and I close my eyes and flinch, but he doesn't hit me. Instead, he sits on the bed and wraps his meaty arms around me and pulls me in for a bear hug. I resist but he just tightens his arms. After an awkward second the dam I built up to hold back the tears bursts and I start sobbing. This is the first time someone has offered me comfort and compassion in days. I wrap my arms around his waist and cry. I cry for Charlotte, for me, for us and the future that we may never have.

He says quietly to me, "This isn't your fault. No one thinks that."

"Her father does. Everyone does. Nobody says it, but they are thinking it," I sniffle back.

"No, he doesn't. I spoke to him," he replies and I scoot back to look up at him. "It was an accident. He believes she can be found and rescued. We believe it too or we wouldn't have flown halfway around the world to help you. Have some faith that God has protected her and we will find her."

"I know that God has kept her safe. I know the scriptures about angels protecting us, but I honestly don't feel them right now," I reply.

He lets me go and steps back, crossing his arms again. He's quiet until I look at him. He grins, "Since when did your feelings change God's plans?" He pauses for an answer and raises one eyebrow. "Be downstairs in five minutes or I'll carry you down like a little girl." He winks at me and blows me a kiss, walking out with a chuckle.

The last few minutes have been surreal. I need to get moving before the big guy follows through on his threat. I walk into the bathroom and splash water on my face and stare into the mirror. I speak to God, "Just for the record, I don't like any of this. But here we are. I know You're good and in control, so, without sounding too bossy, I need You to show up big right now and help me get my wife back."

Downstairs the Rangers are standing by the front desk of the lodge. They seem to be arguing with the clerk and I'm nervous to find out what the problem is. The man who talked to me in my room, who I assume is the leader, is leaning over the counter toward the clerk, on his elbows, obviously applying some physical intimidation.

"Sir, please understand, there is nothing I can do," the clerk pleads with his palms pressed together as if praying for help. "The pilot for the prop plane does not work for us. You and I have no control over his schedule. You heard the phone call. He is making repairs to the plane today and it will not be ready for flight until tomorrow morning."

The Ranger leans back and pounds the counter with a fist. He takes a deep breath then turns to the group. "No flight today. We will be leaving," he turns and glares at the clerk, "at daybreak tomorrow." Everyone shakes their heads in disbelief. It's been one delay after another. "In case it hasn't occurred to you, we are fighting a spiritual war. Every battle is won by faith and praising God for the victory even before we see it. There will be zero negativity or anxiety allowed." I get a long look after this statement. "We will make the best of our time for training and exercise." He gives us the smile of a Cheshire cat right before it eats the mouse. Oh boy.

Chapter 17

Day 15

"*God is fearsome— everything in the cosmos fits and works in his plan.*"
Job 25:1 MSG

Today I wake up with some positive energy. Excited is not the right word because my circumstances don't really allow that. I think purposeful is the best way to describe how I feel. My morning routine seems to take a little longer because I'm eager to get started . I grab my "slate" as I like to think of it and carry it over to the cave paintings. I have to be careful because to make it light enough to carry, it makes it more prone to breaking. If I were to drop this, it would shatter. This feels like doing the "Four R's" on a slate tablet in a one room schoolhouse except if I broke it there I would get my hands smacked with a ruler.

I get to the cave painting and sit down with my legs outstretched, resting the slate on my thighs. Suddenly it occurs to me that I have nothing to write with. Head slap. I gingerly set the rock aside and look for something to draw with. I find some pieces of rock about the size of the black lava rock like used in landscaping. When I take one back to the slate, it doesn't make even the faintest scratch on it. It crumbles in my hands. After immaturely throwing the rocks at the wall, I plop down and lean against a boulder.

I'm stumped. There are no other rocks to try. As I examine the paintings I notice that the cave painters used a lighter colored material also. I walk around looking for light-colored rocks and minerals. Most of them are just basic gray from the limestone. There are some pretty streaks of sparkly quartz, gypsum and some granite mixed in. I rubbed my hands over the walls and all the other surfaces feeling for any residue that the rocks would leave on my hand. After several minutes, all I have is gray dust. I go back to the cave painting and sit down, looking at it and trying to think. The lighter color is an off-white, but I don't know if it was actually originally pure white and aged overtime or if the material was originally off-white. I go with the first theory that it was white and aged. Now I need to search again and look specifically for anything white. I shake my head because this should've been obvious in the first place. I am limited on where I can search, but I don't see any streaks or any areas where white dust or powder rub off.

I'm getting frustrated because I'm losing my light and what I thought was going to start as a productive day has turned out to be unproductive. Like the saying, one step forward and two steps back. I'm getting a headache and I know I need to stop, and step back so that I can get some clarity. I head back to the pool for a break. After lunch, I'm frustrated and overwhelmed, so I lay back and try to clear the emotion out so that I can think. I fall asleep and pass the rest of the day in this depressed slump. This experience is an emotional roller coaster and the end of the ride seems to be nowhere in sight.

Kevin

The last leg of the journey went smoothly and our prop plane took off at first light and landed in Lukla with enough time left to get settled in for the night. Sita greets us at front door of the lodge.

"Mr. Kevin! So good to see you again although I wish for better reasons." She turns to the Rangers, "And these nice young men must be your search team from America. Welcome, welcome." Sita motions for us to follow her inside. "Come, come. I will get Pelo to help you with all your bags. I bet you all would like a cup of hot tea before bed."

"Thank you, Sita, for everything."

She places her palms together over her heart and gives a small bow of her head. "Anything for you, Mr. Kevin. You are family." She smiles and asks the group, "Now which of you big soldiers is the leader?" There are some chuckles and comments arguing about who the biggest is.

Rick glares at them and clears his throat. "That would be me, ma'am. Rick is the name. Pleasure to make your acquaintance. Thank you for your hospitality."

She replies, "Anything for Kevin. Pelo was asking to speak with you this evening and go over previous search efforts."

"Perfect," he replies. I'll sit over here in the dining room with a cup of your fine tea and wait for him."

Pelo comes out and they go over the previous trip. They have us all sit in a circle while Pelo recounts the history and mythology of the mountain. It is a productive meeting, and we will be prepared to start early tomorrow morning.

Things have been so rushed and intense. I tell Rick and the team that I'm going to my room for some quiet time. He raised his eyebrows at me and I could practically hear the cogs in his brain spinning, thinking that I shouldn't be alone in my emotional sate.

"Guys, I know I've been a drama queen that last few days." Heads nod in agreement from everyone. "I need some quiet time alone to recharge my batteries. The only way to do that is time alone with God. I'm going to my room to read and pray then get a good night's sleep." I raise both hands up in surrender. "If you're worried about my mental health, you're more than welcome to check on me later."

Rick gives me one of those manly hand shake/back thumps. "My man. We're here if you need anything."

My morning devotions have always been a cornerstone in my life, but the craziness of the last couple weeks has kept me from having any quiet time with God. Boy, can I tell the difference when I haven't been in the Word for a while. People generally think I'm a nice person, but honestly I can't be loving, patient, kind and forgiving without God. It just doesn't come natural to us as humans. I simply can't be the man I'm supposed to be without reading my Bible and praying every day. I'm not super religious about it, though. I fully believe Christianity is a relationship and I view scripture reading and prayer as having a conversation with God. Reading the Bible is listening to God and prayer is talking to him.

When I don't know what to read, I go to the Psalms. David is brutally honest about his feelings with God. I can relate to that. I pull up my Bible app and find Psalm 91. I read it out loud then re-read it over and over, speaking those words to God. I recite them as a prayer over Charlotte. The scriptures give me words to pray when I don't even know where to start. "Because she loves me, says the Lord, I will rescue her." I'm holding on to this promise. God promises to command his angels to watch over us wherever we go. Wherever Charlotte is at, she is most likely struggling with her faith too, but I know she loves God. She never stopped. And God doesn't give up on people.

"Just hold on Char," I whisper. "Help is on the way."

Chapter 18

Day 16

"God met me more than halfway, he freed me from my anxious fears."
Psalm 34:4 MSG

"Why do I do this?" I mentally scream as I wake up. I am sore and stiff from falling asleep yesterday by the pool. I'm disgusted that I wasted yet another day without getting any closer to escaping. But more than anything, I'm determined. I am not going to die in this cave. I know there is a way out; I can feel it. I don't think my extra sleep was entirely wasted because while I was asleep my unconscious brain figured out a solution. First, I think the reason I haven't found anything because I was looking for the wrong thing. Second, I haven't even search the entire cave; I just gave up after a few half-hearted hours searching. Finally, to recreate the "paint" these people used, I need to think like them.

I eat breakfast and think while I chew. How did these ancient people draw in here? I know they used some form of black medium that I can't seem to find. I also have not figured out what rocks they used for the off-white markings. "Help me Lord," I sigh. The solution is just out of reach. It feels like a dream from the night before that I only vaguely remember.

I walk over to the painting and examine a line closely. There's something in the line that I hadn't noticed before. It's like there's a lot of starts and stops as opposed to a smooth line. The line is almost the exact width of my finger. Then it hits me, the off-white color was finger painted on. They didn't have paint so they must have made paint. I doubt they had containers to bring with them on their hike up the mountain, which might mean that they made the paint in here. If they could make paint then I can too.

Paint is a mixture of a solid powder and a liquid, either water or oil. Clay would be a perfect medium for the base, but it would not show up on the cave wall so something needed to be added to it to lighten it. I think back to my walk around the cave for what light-colored materials I saw. Quartz and granite would be too hard to crush, but gypsum is easily crushed and is actually one of the ingredients for drywall. I know this because Kevin worked finishing drywall when we were dating and would be completely covered with a fine white powder after work.

I race the clock for light again in my search for the meaning to the message of the painting. I take my flat rock and a smaller thin one over an area with a gypsum streak. Holding the flat rock like a tray under where I'm going to scrape, and it's heavy one-handed, I scrape the small rock across the vein. A shower of powder floats down onto the rock. I do a little happy dance and keep scraping until I have a small mound of it. "Don't sneeze," I chuckle, feeling a sneeze building up, "or trip." Next I scoop some clay from the ground on the rock too. Now the light has moved on and I carefully walk back to the pool, watching where I step.

After making it safely back to the pool, I study my rock and mentally plan the best way to mix my paint. I'm going to have to find or make a vessel to mix it in and transport it. After I eat lunch, I begin to walk around looking for small rocks that have a curved shape or a cup or bowl-like feature. There are surprisingly few loose rocks throughout the cave, which I assume is from very little erosion. I keep walking around the cave, and as the afternoon light moves towards the far end of the cave, I find a rock that has a hole in it caused by water dripping on it overtime. It is small, but I can make small batches of paint and I really don't need to make a lot at a time anyway.

I returned to the pool with my paint-mixing rock. I spend the rest of the day working on the formula for the paint. I need to get the right ratio of clay to gypsum to water. I don't have anything to measure with so I just add large pinches of the clay and gypsy powder into what I now consider my bowl. I start adding drops of water and mixing it with my finger. At first, it's a paste, but as I add a drop at a time into it, it liquefies into a thick liquid with the consistency of a thick paint like primer.

I practice with my first batch of paint on some rocks around the pool. It is very slow going, but it feels good to have a form of self-expression. I didn't realize how much I had missed writing and drawing, even if it is silly doodles. I used to draw a lot in my younger years until I became focused on my career. I miss the days of sitting in the grass outdoors and drawing and painting nature scenes. So much can be learned by studying nature. God's creation reveals to us what he is like. I use up the rest of my paint and wash my hands and the bowl in the pool. It's time to close up shop for the day and get rested for tomorrow. Finally, a productive day.

Kevin

I don't have to be dragged out of bed this morning. Getting a full night of restful sleep does wonders. I wake up and read Psalm 91 again and pray for God's protection for our group heading out. After gathering up my gear, I walk down to the lobby to meet up with the rest of the team.

Now that I'm coherent enough to process what's going on, I see that the Rangers have made a very strategic plan for our search. I set down my pack with the rest by the door and head over to the table where they are sitting with maps and numerous coffee cups. The Ranger who helped me yesterday is sitting in the center and he gives me a manly nod as I come over.

"Morning, Kev," he greets me.

"Good morning," I reply with a big exhale. There's an awkward pause and all eyes are on me. They are obviously waiting on me to say something more. "I'm sorry for the last few days. Forgive me. They have been rough." I pause and run a hand through my hair. "I've been so out of it. I'm so ashamed; you all have flown halfway around the world with me and I don't even know your names. Care to bring me up to speed?" I ask.

The man from yesterday stands up. "Of course. By the way, no apology needed. I'm not sure any of us would have done better in your situation." He looks around and they all nod their heads in agreement. "We are the Ranger Alpine Rescue Team, RART, trained to locate and rescue mountain hikers and skiers. We also occasionally track down and capture or eliminate enemy targets. Charlotte's father called in a favor and got permission to activate us to find Charlotte. My name is Rick and I'm the lead on this mission. With me are Gunther, Omar, Chad, and Little John." Each nods when he lists off their names. "We have a very high success rate and feel confident about this mission." He looks at me and I nod and motion for him to continue.

"The plan is simple. Hike up the mountain, search the area she was last seen and rescue Charlotte. The details are a little more complicated. We have clearance for a one-week operation, meaning up and down, before we have to fly back to the States for our next operation. This time window is not negotiable. If you have basic math skills, you've figured out that means three days up, a full day of searching, and three days down. To maximize our time we will have to be efficient and disciplined, not only in searching but in the logistics of mountain hiking and conserving resources." He pauses, obviously wanting confirmation of his explanations.

"I'm tracking so far," I tell him. "Three up, three down, one day to search. No accidents or delays, I assume?"

"Correct. We do not have any spare time for accidents and injuries. Not only are we on a schedule, but time is paramount in a rescue. The longer she is stranded, the lower her survival rate. She could be hurt, dehydrated, and even in poor mental health. We must be efficient but not reckless. In our business, fast can be fatal. On a different topic, how familiar are you with a handgun?"

"I grew up hunting and in a family of proud NRA members," I answer.

"My man," he replies with a fist bump. He hands me a nine millimeter in a holster that clips to my belt. I nod and clip it on. Once in position, the weight of it on my hip actually makes me feel more confident. I stand a little straighter. I think to myself, we're going to do this.

"You are currently the expert on this hike because you have been up the mountain twice." He points to the topographical map laid out on the table. Pointing at it, "We're here. The trail is marked on this line with the lookout that you didn't make it to up here. We were told you had hiked a full day then half of the second day." I nod. "You told the guides that you estimated it at fifteen miles up the trail."

"That was my best guess. The first day of hiking was easier because the trail wasn't as steep so we covered a lot of ground. The second day was rougher and it was starting to get harder to breathe, which is why we took a long break."

"We will be going probably twice as slow as you did, fanning out as we hike up," he explains, "which is why we allowed for three up and down."

"That's pretty much what the guides did too," I reply.

"By the door you'll see piles for gear. Each person carries a GPS, radio, one-man tent, sleeping bag, first aid supplies, water, water purification tablets, seven days of MREs and granola bars, along with coats and boots and other outerwear gear. Let's pray then we'll get loaded up. We need to cover at least five miles today, preferably seven, but we don't want to rush it. Gather up."

Everyone stands up and we make a circle wrapping our arms around each others' shoulders. "Kevin, would you like to pray?" I shake me head no. "No problem. God, thank You for this day, for waking us up. You are good and big and loving. Guide us today, protect us, surround us with Your angels. Give us wisdom during this mission. And most of all, be with Charlotte. Comfort and protect her. We give You all the glory now for her rescue, and everyone in agreement said..." We all say amen together. The guys all put their hands in the middle like a football huddle. "Charlotte on three." I slap my hand on top. "One. Two. Three. Charlotte!" Everyone breaks. They clap it out and load up.

Chapter 19

Day 17

"When things are bad, we take comfort in the thought that they could always get worse. And when they are, we find hope in the thought that things are so bad they have to get better."
Malcom S. Forbes

I've heard it said that being self-employed is the hardest job you'll ever have. I never believed that because I've had a lot of hard jobs, both physically and mentally. In high school I mowed yards, worked fast food and waitressed. Once I graduated college I was able to get a job as a bank teller until I got on as an intern at Penn Financial Group. My current situation is similar to running a small business. However, based on my job performance in this cave, if I was the boss I would have fired me already. It's not like me to be lazy, have little motivation and a bad attitude. I lay around on the job when I should be productive.

I roll out of my mossy bed and stretch. I'm getting used to it but some days are harder than others, especially if I was active the day before. Walking around in a cave isn't exactly aerobic exercise, but it does require a lot of balance and coordination, as I have learned the hard way, twice. I hope that when I leave that I'll be lighter on my feet and more flexible. Doing more yoga if and when I escape is high on my list of things I need to change in my life.

I want to get moving quickly so I munch on my breakfast as I mix up paint. This batch of paint uses up all of my clay and gypsum powder so I will need to scrape some more after I paint the symbol. I'll need to find another rock for tomorrow. This paint sets up quickly so once it is mixed I walk quickly over to the paintings and sit down with my flat rock on my lap and the bowl of paint beside me. For some reason I'm nervous. Like copying the symbols down makes it real. What makes it real is that I believe they mean something. I can't think about it too long because the cynical part of my brain will talk me out of this. I firmly remind it that I am currently trapped in a cave so just about anything is possible.

I dip my finger in the paint and make my first line of the symbol. It is a horizontal line. Then I paint a symbol similar to a W above it. I look at my symbol and compare it to the wall. Theirs is better of course; it's more fluid. But you could pick it out in a police line-up. Even though this is a simple design it takes several minutes to finish. I try to be careful while working as quick as I can before all my paint dries.

I take my painted rock back to the pool and set it down where I won't trip on it or splash it. I wash my hands and the bowl before the remaining paint dries and cakes up my bowl. I eat some lunch and examine the symbol. It feels good to study it without having a time limit. I have a prickly feeling like I've seen this somewhere before or at least one similar to it. A wave of grief hits me as I wish again for the millionth time that Kevin was with me, though preferably not here in this cave. I know we could survive something like this together. He doesn't get rattled when life is hard. The roots of his faith go deep and have supported me many times. My trust in God has become stronger through these trials. I'm excited to see where God takes us if and when I get out.

Conviction grips my spirit. God is telling me I need to stop saying, "If I get out." There is no halfway trusting God, so I throw caution to the wind and tell God, "It's official. I believe you will rescue me or show me how to escape. Help me to trust you more. I can't wait to see how you're going to show off big in my life. Wherever Kevin I pray you strengthen him from the inside out. Give him the spiritual fortitude to never give up. Somehow someway show him I'm still alive and love him dearly."

Kevin

This is now my third trip hiking up the mountain trail. The first time was exciting, an adventure with Charlotte. The second time was a climb of desperation. I was manic with anxiety, fearing the worst. It was painful to hope, but I wasn't going to give up on her. This trip, however, is not an adventure or a crazy rescue mission. It is a precise, calculated operation. Watching these men do their job is like being in an action movie. I've resented Charles many times over the years for his inability to turn off "The General," as I jokingly call him to Charlotte, but I'm thankful for his ability to get these Rangers' help. Their confidence is reassuring, and I need all the positive vibes I can get.

Rick and his teammates head out with the only one instruction: "Standard procedures, boys."

This was followed immediately with, "Yes, sirs," from the team in unison.

Rick instructed me when we left, "You have two jobs. First is to tell me every detail of your hike with Charlotte. Leave nothing out. Second is most important: do not leave my side, for any reason."

I nod my head in agreement. The miles went by slower than I was used to and we hiked every minute of daylight. We made it a little over six miles before we had to stop for the day and set up camp for the night. The team was all business tonight: tents, food, sleep. I lay in my tent praying for a dreamless sleep. Being on this mountain again was definitely triggering me.

I see movement outside my tent followed by someone saying, "Knock, knock."

"Come in?" I reply, wondering which Ranger it might be and why. The zipper slides down with a puff of cold air. It's Rick.

"Hey, buddy. I was just checking if you had been able to fall asleep yet."

"No, not yet, obviously." I replied with a weak smile that he probably couldn't see in the dark.

"I was worried that might be the case. I though a bedtime story might help," he replies with a chuckle. I roll my eyes, thankful he couldn't see that. "Every mission RART goes on is top secret so I can't share any of our stories. However, I know of a group of handsome, highly trained soldiers who have a worldwide reputation for rescuing kidnap victims out of the clutches of evil, violent terrorists." At this I laugh. "What?" He laughs too. "I'm laying it on thick, huh?"

"Keep going. It feels good to laugh," I tell him.

"On one special mission the soldiers had to climb high into the Afghani mountains to rescue the child of the ambassador who had been kidnapped. They found him in a cave with a terrorist holding a gun to his head."

"Wow!" I reply, completely absorbed in the story. "What did you, I mean they, do?"

"Of course they tried to talk and reason with the terrorists first, but it turns out that terrorists aren't all that reasonable. Then the soldiers gave the terrorists an ultimatum: release the boy or everyone dies. The soldiers were outnumbered three to one and each terrorist had an AR. The leader counted out loud down from ten then," he pauses.

I finish his sentence. "The soldiers mow them all down."

"God no! That would make for an awful diplomatic mess. No, a successful Ranger mission is one that doesn't make headlines. The leader shot the terrorist holding the boy in the foot which made him drop his gun. Another soldier grabbed the boy and the rest of the team secured the terrorists in plasti-cuffs."

I sigh. "Bummer. I hoping for a lot more action than that."

He laughs, "Oh, there's plenty of those but they wouldn't help you sleep. I just wanted you to know that RART has successful experience in rescuing people in bad situations very similar to this."

I give him a thumbs up. "Message received." I yawn, "Thanks, I feel like I'm going to pass out and sleep like a log now."

"Glad to help, buddy." He exits the tent and pulls the zipper back down.

I whisper, "Thank you God for these men. Not only are they helping rescue Charlotte, but I think they just might be making me a better man."

Chapter 20

Day 18

"There's more to come: We continue to shout our praise even when we're hemmed in with troubles, because we know how troubles can develop passionate patience in us, and how that patience in turn forges the tempered steel of virtue, keeping us alert for whatever God will do next. In alert expectancy such as this, we're never left feeling shortchanged. Quite the contrary— we can't round up enough containers to hold everything God generously pours into our lives through the Holy Spirit!"
Romans 5:5 MSG

I wake up so excited at my progress yesterday. I study the symbol I painted while I munch on breakfast. I'm looking forward to painting the second one today. After stretching and eating, I get ready to make more paint, but it occurs to me that I don't have any more rocks to paint on. I groan. I can't believe I forgot to get another rock! I am going to have to wait until this afternoon to go over there to make more rock canvases. That leaves me without a plan for the morning.

I feel a little lost and it really deflates my balloon real quick, but I have to keep the negative thoughts away. I remember the scripture in James, I think, "If anyone lacks wisdom let him ask of the Lord and He will give it generously." I ask God to tell me what I can do this morning. Talking to God, or "praying" as the church people like to call it, is now interwoven into my daily routine. I talk to Him like he's right here in this cave with me. I don't hear his voice audibly, but I get ideas from things he has whispered in my heart.

I feel like I need to spend time updating my notes I've been writing on the floor. It's much like a detective with their boards that have all the details of a case and how they connect. First I update my hash marks; it's been eighteen-days. The enormity of that is astounding both in how long I've been down here but also in how long God has provided for me. It's kind of like the proverbial question of whether the glass is half full or empty.

Next I add to the facts section: five symbols, similar to hieroglyphics or Chinese characters, in a line much like the ones in the Egyptian pyramids that Kevin took me to. I don't know what they mean yet, but my gut tells me that it is a message or instructions for how to get out of this cave.

By the time I finish all this the light has moved to where I can start breaking off sections of rock for the remaining symbol paintings. I don't see any the perfect size laying around like a couple days ago. I do see a rock with a point and it use it like a chisel. I use a bigger rock like a hammer to break away thin flat canvases. This is delicate work and I break several before I get four of them in the shape and size I need. My hands have blisters and scrapes with lots of dust caked in. I carry two rocks at a time back to the pool, carefully. Breaking one would set me back another day. Tired and hungry I sit beside the pool and wash my hands in the water. Moments later my hands are clean and healed. I shake my head and thank God for taking care of me. I had skipped lunch and eating dinner makes me tired. I crawl into bed with thanksgiving on my lips.

It's so important to say the things I'm thankful for out loud. Something about hearing it makes it more real. "Thank you God for keeping me alive. I don't know why I'm here but I know you are good and loving. Thank you for Kevin and please keep him safe. Thank you for my parents. Help me restore our relationships when I get out. Thank you for my job. I might need to adjust my work load but I mostly enjoy it. And finally and most importantly, thank you Jesus for your forgiveness. I don't know where I would be without you. Probably dead, or in a mental hospital or jail." My words fade out as I drift off to sleep.

Kevin

At first light we break down camp, eat our breakfast bars and drink some very cold water. Rick pulls out the map while Omar pulls up his GPS. They compare and discuss today's hike. Rick tells us, "The hike is getting harder because of elevation and altitude. Each mile we cover allows us more time for searching when we get there. My goal is for us to hike another six miles today, but it will take more stamina so dig deep." I shoulder my pack and take my gloves off to retie my boots. It's getting colder but the brisk hiking warms me as long as we keep moving. My feet have blisters from so much hiking in a short time period, but it barely compares to the pain in my heart.

Rick keeps us encouraged and pushes us hard to keep going. My thighs are burning and knees and ankles ache, but he is a consummate source of positivity. He's like my high school football coach giving us a pep talk in the last quarter on fourth down at the five yard line with three seconds left.

Rick told me at one point, "Most of us don't truly know what we are fully capable of because we've never been in a situation where we had to give one hundred percent. It's like the mother who can pick a car up off of her child or a fireman running into a burning building to save his friend. This is your moment. What you do now will change the course of you life forever. Dig deep. I believe your pursuit is a big factor in saving her." He turns and grabs me by the shoulder, looking me dead in the eye. "It's not over till it's over. Capiche?"

I nod and beat my chest with my fist. "It's not over," I repeat. We ground out a grueling seven miles today. I ask God to my faith as solid and unmoving as the mountain we climb. I pray fervently for Charlotte to keep holding on. Back at my tent, the exhaustion from the hike today and the spiritual battle I'm fighting make falling asleep easy effortless.

Chapter 21

Day 19

"It takes but one positive thought when given a chance to survive and thrive to overpower an entire army of negative thoughts."
Robert H. Schuller

I wake up with determination to get the second symbol painted. After my morning routine, I mix up more paint in my bowl and take it and a rock canvas over to the cave painting. The second symbol from the right looks a like an eye, notably a right eye, based on the tear duct being on the left. It is oval shaped with a wing on the outside tip. There is a slightly curved eyebrow above the eye and the pupil is a solid circle. Under the lower lid is a hooked line and another short straight line descending from the tear duct. I have to paint this large because of the detail and how wide my finger is. It would be much easier with paintbrush or marker or better yet, just snap a picture with a camera or phone. I know there is an app that lets you upload a picture and it can identify a plant or a bird. Surely there is one for symbols and hieroglyphs, too. Maybe these symbols are even still in use in cultures somewhere in the world. That's an interesting thought.

I let my brain process all these things while I dip my finger and paint. Sometimes the best way to think about something is to not think about it. Kevin taught his students that, technically speaking, your brain remembers everything that it is exposed to, but it has limitations on how much it can process at one time. Like computers, it will compress files that aren't used frequently and store them away to make more room for new information and faster processing. He would tell them that you have to help your "computer" access those files, but this often proves to be difficult to do by simply asking it for the answer directly.

A person has to be able to call up that information much like how you use keywords to search for pictures or files. In our brain, however, those key words can be attached to emotions; for example: positive, joyful, negative, abusive, and especially traumatic events. Facts and events can be triggered by music, smell, loud sounds, and even lights. This area of brain research, he told me, is only in its infancy and has unlimited potential for people from all walks of life and careers.

I finish the last line of the eye and examine my work. It's intense. The eye is staring at me. I have to look away, like when you're in a staring contest and I lost the game. The eye doesn't seem evil, in fact I feel safer. Maybe it's watching out for me. I start singing, "I'll be watching you."

I carry the finished painting back to the pool. I set it beside the first rock painting then rinse my hands and clean out the bowl. I feel like I've accomplished something today. It is my firm conviction that these symbols go together and have a message in them. I'm exhausted, and the day is only half gone, but I don't have the energy to do even one more thing. I sit beside the pool on a flat, mossy rock and dangle my feet in, munching on some greens.

My hiking boots didn't survive the journey down the cave with me, and my socks gave up the ghost after the first day of walking in this rocky cave so I've been barefoot this whole time. My feet have some tough callouses and many scrapes and bruises. My heels feel like eighty-grit sandpaper. It's been a few days since my swim, and I've accumulated some new scrapes and bruises since then. I roll up my pant legs and sit on the edge of the pool with my legs in the water up to my knees. Leaning back on my elbows, I close my eyes at the pleasure. I want to bottle it up. The healing power from the pool is like having dozens of goldfish nibbling on my feet. It tickles, which makes me giggle. I almost want to pull them out because my feet are so ticklish but I keep them in and let God do his thing.

These moments by the pool are extraordinary—they leave me speechless every day. All I can find to say is, "Thank you Lord." Telling God thanks is the biggest part of my conversation with him. "Thank you Lord for your provision, again. I might be lost and alone, but I'm not forgotten."

The agenda for the afternoon is a lazy nap. Just what I need. Above ground I used to feel guilty about taking naps. I knew I needed to rest but as soon as I closed my eyes a slideshow started playing in my head of everything I should be doing. This new Cavewoman can lie here on a bed of reeds and moss and drift off to sleep in moments like a baby. Lying here now on my pallet I watch the light twinkle in the ceiling, falling asleep and wondering how Kevin is doing.

"Lord, protect him, and let him know that you're taking care of me," I mumble before falling asleep.

Kevin

The sounds of tents being packed up stirs me awake, and I roll over and groan. Everything hurts. I sit up and have to take some long, deep breaths to suppress the pain. I've hiked over seventy miles in two and a half weeks. I'm trying my hardest not to whine, but surely if anyone was given a free pass to complain it would be me. I roll my neck and stretch my arms over my head, leaning left and right, then twist my back until it cracks and the tension starts to leave.

I look up at the inside point of my tent and whisper, "God, I need You. I can't go on without your help. Give me strength, patience, and courage most of all. Be with

Charlotte and give her the strength to hold on." I take a minute to recite Psalm twenty-three, Charlotte's favorite, a few times until the words bring me peace. "The Lord is my shepherd; I shall not want..."

"Alright, let's do this!" I'm ready to start the day. I pack up my tent, sleeping mat and bags then join the team.

"Final push today," Rick says. "Pelo and Kevin have warned us that these last few miles are more difficult. Very rocky. Some places are more climbing than hiking. Several switchbacks. We may have to take breaks because we will breathing harder while the oxygen is getting thinner. It's better to take a break than pass out. Just let the person closest to you know if you need to rest. Let's pray."

Rick always prays like he's talking to God, a conversation between family or friends. His simple faith is encouraging. These big bulky soldiers aren't too macho to share and live their faith. I want to be a big bulky soldier who loves God like they do when I grow up.

Two miles on a near vertical trail makes for slow-going. There's no way to spread out any more; we are single file now. Less trees and more boulders. It's just a narrow snowy trail weaving up a rock face. The wind stings and the snow is powdery making for treacherous footing.

When we popped over the top of the last rock, the ground flattens out into a little clearing, just as I remembered from my first hike. It's a welcome reprieve from the strenuous hike. I remember Charlotte telling me it reminded her of the Dolly Sods wilderness in Canaan Valley, West Virginia. You drive up over these mountains down into this flat, lush green plateau that is literally a different ecosystem. It's more like Canada than Appalachia. There is still some snow here from the last storm, but I can see the bushes and trees that dot the clearing. Large boulders that have rolled down the top of the mountain are scattered around. I collapse after cresting the final rock: I'm so relieved to be on flat ground. The Rangers also sit or squat to rest as they come up.

"This is it," I say, out of breath.

Rick and the Rangers look around the clearing. Mountains surround it on three sides so that from the lodge you can't see it because they are always in the clouds.

"If I believed in magic I would say this was a magical place," John says while exploring the clearing.

"I know! Like I can imagine a battle like in <u>Lord of the Rings</u> between the orcs and dwarves happening here," Gunther chimes in. His LOTR reference takes me by surprise.

John replies, "The elves always have to come help the dwarves even though they hate each other."

I'm staring open-mouthed at these two big Rangers casually joking about Lord of the Rings. Then Rick joins, "What's that in your pocketesss?"

At this I laugh and shake my head. "That's enough, hobbits."

"Let's rest a bit then we'll continue," Rick tells us as he slings his back down.

We sip at our water canteens and catch our breath. Rick turns to me, "Lead us across the Shire to where you last saw Charlotte." I'm glad he's adding some humor to this because I'm getting very anxious. This is it. Either we find her in the next day and a half or we don't.

"Follow me. Over this way," I tell them and we walk across the clearing. My hands are trembling and heart is like a hummingbird's. I walk over and stand where Charlotte and I stopped to eat lunch. You can see where we cleared rocks to make a place to sit. John and Chad start looking at the area then go off the right while Omar and Gunther check around the other sides.

"I can tell this is hard for you, but I need you to stay calm and give me the facts. Show me where Charlotte walked to," Rick tells me. I point to the left where a large juniper bush is.

"She went behind that bush to go to the bathroom. I could see her just a little through the branches of this bush. It looked like she jumped up like this," I reenact jumping with arms straight, "with her ponytail flipping up too. She squealed then everything was quiet and she was gone." I whisper. "I found her watch in some dirt beside a large rock that's right behind it."

"Gotcha." He whistles and the team comes over. They spread out to make a straight line. Each one has fancy sticks that they tap the ground with before taking a step forward. I'm behind Rick. As we get around the bush, the rock comes into sight. We proceed to the rock then stop. Chad steps forward and places an electronic device that looks like a multimeter on top of the rock. He adjusts some knobs then shakes his head. "It's strange. I've never seen these types of readings in all of my testing." He taps the ground around the rock with his stick then tests several spots with the meter also. "The rock and ground have high levels of magnetic residue, but it's impossible to tell without more extensive research if this is within the normal parameters for this region. The soil around it seems to be completely normal. It's almost as if this rock doesn't belong in this area, like it somehow moved from another location."

The scientist in me is intrigued. I've used a lot of high tech equipment but this one is new to me. I bend down next to him. "What does that measure?"

Rick answers, "Oh, this is a top secret tool that Chad developed. It can detect seismic, magnetic, electric activity while recording abnormalities in temperature and geologic formations. This is a prototype he developed for the Army. It will help detect IEDs and could save many soldiers' lives. In alpine rescue application it has been highly successful."

"Wow!" I raise my eyebrows. "When you say "geologic abnormalities" you mean man-made features," I interject.

"Exactly. When people are lost on mountains it can be from rock slides, for example, which are triggered by some form of activity. We need to determine if the spot a person disappeared at was disturbed by natural causes or by man. That will gives us information for which way the person was moved," Rick explained.

There is a pause where we are all staring at the ground. Chad is still moving the tools around and adjusting settings. He stands up and wipes his hands on his pants.

"Unfortunately, we are not getting enough data to get a definitive answer, but something abnormal happened here," Chad tells us.

"Abnormal describes my last three weeks." My face must give away how I'm feeling.

"There's one more tool we need to try out," Chad says. He digs around in his bag and pulls out something that looks like a walking stick that has been folded in thirds. He unfolds it and attached a spade to the tip then holds it up to me. "Technology is great but we always need to remember to examine things tactually. Use the five senses. We will start in the area you found the watch."

Chad hands the small shovel to John and points to where he wants him to start. He pulls out a sleeping mat and lays it beside the spot. He turns to me, "If you were excavating this for a dig how would you proceed, keeping in mind our limited equipment, time and other resources?"

I take one of the sticks and draw a square in the dirt with the tip, then smaller squares within it, each being about the width of a shovel. "Start in a corner and dig out each square. Chad and I will study the dirt you dug out, and the rest of you can examine the hole," I instruct.

John digs straight down around the edges of the first square then scoops out a perfect block of dirt and deposits it on the mat. Chad motions for me to examine it first. Before touching it I look closely all around then sniff it. I don't want to compact the dirt more so I ask for tweezers or a small knife. Of course they all have Swiss Army knives which have both tools. I use the small blade to spread out the dirt flat. It is a mixture of top soil and small gravel. After determining that there is nothing foreign in the soil, I move out of the way so Chad can examine. He examines the dirt, then picks up a moist clump, tasting it.

I blurt out, "What in the world?"

Chad holds up a finger indicating just a second. He rolls it in his mouth a second more then spits it in the grass. "Water, please." Omar hands him a water bottle and he swishes a mouthful before spitting it in the grass too. I'm staring at him with eyebrows raised. "If there was blood it would have soaked into the soil and would not be visible any more, but the coppery taste of it will remain much longer than the visible. That's why we use our technology as well as our five senses. Good news, though. No blood."

We continue to examine each quadrant for dirt, digging down one foot in each one. In the center square Chad finds a broken nail with the color nail polish Charlotte was wearing: midnight navy blue. I also find a clump of hairs accompanied by a faint scent of her shampoo. After digging out the entire area we proceed to go deeper but when John sinks in the shovel it only goes a couple inches before hitting rock. We scrape out the last bit of dirt remaining but don't find any more evidence. All that is left is nearly flat granite rock. John takes his shovel around the outside of the square in multiple places with the shovel hitting rock a little over a foot down.

I sit down beside the square we dug out. I would say we hit a wall, but we actually hit a rock. She was here, then she wasn't. "Don't jump to conclusions, Kevin," Rick tells me. There is always a scientific reason for the things that happen."

I point to the hole. "Except for when there isn't," I retort. I put my head in my hands. It is pounding and I feel the sinus pressure building from holding back tears.

He kneels down beside me and pats my back. "We still have all day tomorrow to search for her. Don't give up yet. It's going to be dark soon so let's get back to camp and wind down for the night. It's been a long day."

I nod and get up, taking my gear over to the clearing to set up my tent. I need rest, but I don't know how I can when my mind is whirling. After we eat I crawl into my tent and pray the only thing I have the words for, "God, help me. I can't do this without you. Keep Charlotte safe." Breathe in and out through my nose Charlotte would tell me now if she could. I slow my breathing down to calm the anxiety. "Even though I walk through the valley of the shadow of death, I will fear no evil for you are with me." I feel a warm blanket of serenity rest on me, then I collapse into dreamless sleep.

Chapter 22

Day 20

"You cannot think negative and have a positive life. Meaning you cannot sow tomato seeds and expect pepper fruits."
Oscar Bimpong

Above ground, when I would have a busy day of work ahead of me, I felt most confident if I could get an early start on the day. I like to be able to get into the office before anyone else to go over reports and make lists and plans for the day. But in this cave, there is no option for getting an early start. The sunlight filtering through the cracks prevents it. So I start my day as normal then make a new batch of paint. I carry it and a new rock over to the cave painting when the light hits it.

The third and middle painting is simpler than the first two. It basically looks like a cross, but the top part is like a teardrop or raindrop upside down. The remaining three parts of the cross left flare out instead of just being straight lines. This symbol out of all of them is the most familiar, even though I can't quite place it. I am able to draw this one more quickly, but I don't have enough paint or time to start the next one. I take my supplies back to the pool and clean up. I decide after lunch that I'll go to the far end of the cave and see if there is any wind coming through the cracks today.

After lunch I weave my way over to the far side of the cave and walk around, holding my hand in front of each of the small cracks in the wall. None of them have any airflow except for the one that is at the very farthest end. It is a small crack, almost more like a hole actually. I can't see inside it farther than an inch. I make mental note of it. I need to come back tomorrow to compare the frequency and pattern of the airflow.

That's enough for today, I feel like I have accomplished a lot and that helps me sleep. I thank God for being with me today and for providing everything I need. As always I ask him to be with Kevin and keep him safe.

Kevin

I didn't know it was possible to be excited about something and dread it at the same time. When I woke I was eager to get moving but there was a ticking clock in the back of my head. There is so much pressure to find her today because if we don't... I can't think that way. We will find her. We have to. I can't climb down this mountain again without her. I won't. After crawling out of my tent I join the Rangers by the morning fire. Omar hands me a steaming mug. I take it and inhale the rich scent of coffee, raising my brows at him. "How did you pull this off with our rationed bottled water?"

"I was scouting early this morning around the clearing and found a crystal clear stream running down between the mountains. Cleanest water on earth, I bet. I always carry instant coffee, just in case," he explains.

Blowing on the steaming cup, I take a cautious sip. "It's so good I could cry. Charlotte and I always brought home coffee from wherever we travelled, apart or together. It was our thing." I get quiet and hang my head. "I bet she hasn't had coffee in a long time either." I laugh, "Imagine how cranky she is right now without caffeine. That woman ran on Diet Coke and coffee." The rest of them chuckle. "For real, though, thanks."

He nods and I walk away, sipping my coffee.

A little later Rick rounds us up and we go over our plan for the day. "We didn't find much yesterday at the spot Charlotte disappeared so we need to expand out. We will each go in a cardinal direction. If you see anything, radio for Chad and Kevin to come check it out. Everyone meet back at camp before sundown."

I get geared up to go, but Kevin grabs my arm. "You are staying here. Someone has to stay put in case there is an emergency. We will radio if we find anything."

I am not happy about this arrangement. At least hiking would burn off my nervous energy, but I agree to follow his orders. I put my pack on the ground and use it as a seat and my sleeping bag as a backrest against a large boulder. I don't know what to do with myself while I sit here waiting. I brought a small journal with me but haven't had time to write in it. I open to the first blank page and stare at it. I don't want to write about how I feel but I need to have an outlet for my emotions. Instead of spewing all the negative garbage I'm feeling right now I focus my thoughts on good memories with Charlotte. I decide to write out all, or as many as I remember starting at the beginning. I let the pen take me down memory lane.

Many pages later, the Rangers reappear. They all report no sign of her, but I don't let it discourage me. The journaling has reminded me of how good God has been to me. He'll take care of this. In fact, God's message to me is clear: He's already taken care of it. The problem all along hasn't been God not protecting Charlotte and helping us find her; the problem has been trusting that he is good and has it all under control.

I pray under my breath, "God help me trust that you are good, that you love us and that you are in control."

Chapter 23

Day 21

My father, always the drill sergeant, liked to bark at me, "If it was easy anybody could do it!" To the "anybodies" out there, they must be tougher than me. This whole experience has been hard, and I fantasize about quitting every day. I have laid down on the cave floor many times just hoping one of the stalactites would fall and impale so I didn't have to do this anymore. Then I feel bad for wishing that.

What would Kevin think? Would my busy career-obsessed parents even miss me? But something always pulls me out of that emotional quicksand. I just have to keep going, one minute at a time. The situation is daunting and overwhelming, but every day I stay alive a battle won. Eventually, all these little successes will add up to a victory, escaping this cave and being re-united with Kevin.

My morning runs smoothly until it doesn't. I didn't even realize that my supply of gypsum power and clay had run out yesterday. I groan. Just when I get some momentum I hit another roadblock. I'll have to scrape more gypsum, but I won't have time to do another painting today. I carry my last two flat rocks over to the section of wall where the gypsum deposit is located. I scrape the gypsum with a rock that has a chisel-like edge. It takes some muscle but it flakes away. I will crush it into powder when I get back to the pool.

Next I take my chisel rock to scrape up clay from the floor. I can scoop it up faster than the gypsum. It's so dry in here that everything is loose and flaky. After I carry the rock with the powder back to the pool, I set it down and use a smooth round rock to crush the flakes into fine powder. Now they are ready to be mixed to-morrow.

I have the rest of the day to study the three symbols I have already finished. I've been so focused on getting them copied that I haven't devoted as much time to decoding them. I have three copied so far: a Chinese looking symbol, a funky-looking eye and cross with a tear drop shape on top. There must be a connection be-tween them.

Eating always helps me think better, so I crunch on a tuber of a plant that I can't identify. It looks like a potato and grows under water, so I call it the "water potato". It's crisp like a radish with very little taste but is great at keeping my belly full. It would surely be considered a "super food" above ground, high in fiber and filled with healthy carbs.

Above ground, when I'm trying to figure out how to land a client, I like to put myself in their shoes. What would I want if I were them? What is motivating me to invest? Applying that logic to my current situation, the first question I need to ask is obvious: what were these people trying to communicate to others who came into this cave? But I also need to know, how did they get here? Is there more than one way to get in and out of the cave? Were they here by accident like me or did they come on purpose?

My head is swimming with questions and a multitude of possibilities. The beginning of pounding in my temples warns me that I need to chill out before I get a migraine. I need to calm my racing thoughts so I head over to update my charts. It has now been twenty-one days. Wow. The first few days felt eternally long, but the rhythm of the sunlight has made the days go quickly. I have slept more in this cave than a lazy sloth.

No number of days will make missing Kevin any easier. I can only pray and trust God to help me.

I pray, "God, I feel like I'm repeating myself over and over, but I need you. I can't do this on my own. Help me find a way out. I'm worried this might be equally hard for Kevin. Please comfort, strengthen and protect him."

Kevin

We didn't find her. I failed again. The Rangers are very frustrated too; it's obvious they're not used to failure. I see them huddled together with confusion on their faces. I feel the same way. It just doesn't make sense. Emotionally, I want to throw a fit and curse and cry. I want to break things or blow something up to vent this anger that has been boiling inside me. But more than that, I want to be a man that she would be proud of. Nothing makes sense, but that doesn't change how I feel about her, so I choose to cherish her in my heart. Love always wins.

With heavy hearts, we pack our tents and bags and start the arduous climb down the mountain. Another fifteen miles back down the mountain, and I could care less if I make it there alive. I swore I wouldn't leave the mountain without her, but the Rangers "leave no man behind."

Every time I get angry or want to cry I just think of a happy memory with her and thank God for the time I had with her. We weren't perfect, but we did love each other. Not everyone can say that. Not everyone experiences love like this, storybook love. I hope she knows how much I loved her. I hope I made her feel loved. My beautiful Charlotte, the queen of my heart.

Chapter 24

Day 22

"There is meaning in every journey that is unknown to the traveler."
Dietrich Bonhoeffer

When I wake up it's abnormally dark in the cave. I wonder at first if I slept away the day, but it doesn't feel like it. There is some weak light shining over on the painting but it is not bright enough to work by. I groan, this is yet another set-back. "I don't have time for this!" I yell. It was June when I fell in the cave, but up on a mountain that doesn't mean anything. At this elevation it's some form of winter year around. Even from the pool I can hear whistling of wind coming through the cracks much more than usual. There must be a serious snowstorm out there. I've spent hours lying on the floor of the cave trying to catch even a tiny glimpse of blue sky and clouds. I haven't seen anything, just gray skies and clouds with occasional breeze accompanied by an eerie whistling. However, even the whistle of the wind reminds me that there is a world outside this cave. Staying focused is my tether line of sanity.

God has provided food, water and shelter, but I miss the outdoors, sun and fresh air. I'm the type of person who likes to sleep with a window cracked at night year round - I need the fresh air. Kevin and I fought over it because his allergies act up when the windows are open. I would begrudgingly close the windows, but I'd get up later and secretly crack it back open by my bed after he fell asleep. That's not very loving of me, but I'm not sorry that I'm not sorry.

It's crunch time - only one week left, and it's strange to think this way. After three weeks one week doesn't seem so long. I still have two symbols to paint and a message to decode. I spent all my spare time yesterday studying the symbols and went to bed with them on my mind. The symbols looked so familiar and finally I remembered one last night. Now I'm happy to have figured out, I think, one of the symbols. I believe it will be the key to helping me understand the entire message. I woke up remembering where I had seen it before. On a trip with Kevin to the pyramids in Egypt many years ago, we studied the hieroglyphics in a newly discovered tomb of a prince during the Old Kingdom era. This symbol from the painting was engraved all over the walls. It was called the ankh symbol. It stuck with me because it looks similar to a cross but these were carved before the Romans ever started using it as a torture device. Pharaohs and kings were many times shown holding one as a key to the afterlife, Kevin told me. This key would open the afterlife to them. This word could mean several things: "key, sun, life." It could also mean "open" due to the loop at the top. These characters would make sense to the author and reader based on the context.

The wind has cooled the cave to where the edges of it are cooler than normal. I am not going to be able to work any more on the paintings or studying the cracks. There's just not enough light. The area around the pool is as warm as normal. I have the idea to work today on collecting more moss for my bed. It is a little squashed. I take a minute to plan out a better arrangement: normal beds have a box spring to support the mattress that provides stability for softer mattress on top. I have rock, which is definitely too hard, but I need something softer yet still supportive. Reeds might work. It's worth a try. I pull some up, breaking off the edible bulb and roots and lay the stalks in a criss cross pattern after removing my sad, squashed moss. After placing four layers it looks like a woven mat. I take a step on it and it crunches. I guess I will have to break it in, just like a normal mattress. Next I collect lily pads, shaking the water off them. I layer lily leaves over the reeds. The big round leaves provide a barrier and I overlap them. A fresh layer of spongy moss completes my new mattress. A bed has never looked so inviting and this thought makes me laugh. I want to flop down on it for a cozy nap but I have to hold off until it dries out some.

Judging by the little light I have left, the day is about over. I eat some of the left over bulbs and leaves from making my bed. My hands are cut up a little from breaking the reeds, but I know just how to fix that. I wash them in the pool and wonder at how mind-boggling God's supernatural provision is. I thank God for sustaining me and ask him to be with Kevin wherever he is. As I drift off to sleep, I close my eyes, andI remember that I heard some rumbling sounds throughout the day, but I'm too tired to try to figure out what that could mean.

Kevin

It's our last day hiking down the mountain and even though I wish I could keep searching, I know it is futile. The sky is dark with rain-clouds, or snow depending on temperature and elevation, so the Rangers are trying to hike quickly to beat the rain. The wind is fierce, screaming like a wounded bobcat. I feel defeat leaving but I'm homesick and completely drained. The Rangers got no complaints from me when we got ready to leave. I am finally ready to go home to our apartment. I want to be with her things and her smell.

The Rangers are hiking down the mountain faster than I can keep up. I'm stumbling from fatigue. My vision is blurring with the edges getting dark. After we've been hiking a couple hours, I let the group know I'm going to hang back a minute to pee. I set my pack down and step off the trail. Before I can finish unzipping my fly the ground vibrates, rumbling like a giant with belly pain. It stops just as quickly as it started, just enough to make you think you imagined it. The leaves on the trees rustle briefly like when the wind blows and a low groan seems to come from nowhere and everywhere all at once. I look around for the source of the sound when suddenly it feels like I'm standing on a moving side-walk. Then my heart leaps into my throat as the ground beneath me disappears.

"Charlotte, I love you," I whisper right before my breath is knocked out of me.

Chapter 25

Day 23

"That which does not kill us makes us stronger."
Friedrich Nietzsche

Growing up, I loved the BBC movie adaptations of C.S. Lewis' <u>Chronicle of Narnia</u>. In the <u>The Silver Chair</u> movie, the protagonists are trapped under a ruined city by an evil witch. The marshwiggle Puddleglum, in a fit of despair, cries out, "I'm a marshwiggle. I need the sun!" This scene has played out in my head many times, and I can relate to his outburst.

Sunlight literally affects us, both physically and mentally. We all know about the Vitamin D stuff but it also helps reduce stress, releases happy hormones, and improves sleep because it synchronize our circadian rhythm. I "know" all these facts because in college I was fascinated with brain research and did a research paper on it. However, knowing and applying are two different things.

Above ground, I work in a cubicle under florescent lights studying stocks and investments, on the phone and computer most of the day, and work long hours. I get home late only to shower, collapse in bed and get up early to do it again. Kevin grumbles at me all the time to slow down and take better care of myself. "You're going to work yourself into an early grave," he warns. Now that I've had weeks to reflect on my life I see that I need to make major life changes when I get out. I pray I get the chance.

Now when a sliver of sunlight streaks through the cracks this morning, I revel in it. I missed the light so much yesterday that today I stand in the spotlight of the sunbeam, letting it shine on my face. It is delicious, like warm honey on my skin. Like I can breathe again. After absorbing the sun like a snake on a rock for a moment, I am motivated to get to work quickly to make up for yesterday. I take my breakfast to-go, which makes me laugh, with my rock and bowl of paint.

Today I will be painting the fourth symbol. It is a vertical rectangle with a line down the middle. There is a line going across the center of the middle line with two hashes on each end; it looks a little like an old wood fence except with one rail instead of two. This painting is straight lines and simpler to paint. I am done more quickly with it than the first three. I have a guess what it could represent, but I need to study it more and compare it to the others. I carry the rock back to the pool carefully. I am actually proud of myself for not having any accidents lately. Yay me.

Back at the pool, I line the four rocks up side by side. I get a tingly feeling that I am getting much closer to figuring out the message in the symbols. Soon. This gives me hope and motivation to keep going. "I'm coming, Kevin," I whisper as a prayer to God and promise to him. "Help me Lord," I beg while studying the rocks.

Lunch is accompanied by pacing. I update my chart to twenty-three days. This brings a flutter of panic in my belly. What if I can't figure out the message before the twenty-eight days run out?

My anxiety won't let up even after a failed attempt of a nap after lunch. I just tossed and turned. Eventually I gave up and walk around to the far side looking for a clue, a sign, anything to give me hope. I find nothing— just more of the same. Groaning in frustration I go back to the pool.

On a hunch I strip and slide down the mossy rocks into the pool. The water feels so good I could cry. I think I will actually miss the pool when I leave. The anxiety starts to squeeze my chest again. All the questions I don't have answers for: What if? When? How? and the dreaded Why? The emotional whirlwind feels like it will drown me. I surrender to the calm, hold my nose and dive down. Once again the beauty underneath is dazzling. When my lungs feel like they're going to burst I kick my way back to the surface, gasping for air. I brush the hair out of my eyes and breathe freely.

The absence of the weight from the anxiety trying to crush me buoys me back to sanity. If I don't worry about my problems, how will they ever get fixed? I have to surrender them to God. I remember the scripture, the best that I can, "Don't worry about anything. Pray about everything. And the peace of God, which surpasses all understanding, will guard your heart and mind in Jesus."

"God, I'm just being honest here, but I don't like the idea of giving you my problems. I love being in control. However, I'm kinda stuck and need your help. So I'm going to sit right here, not like I have any other places to go, and wait for you to help me. I trust you and I'm learning to trust you more each day because you're big and good and loving. Amen."

After my prayer I do some breathing exercises and stretch. I hate that my faith wavers every day, but I think the important thing is that I return to trusting him. He's gaining my trust more every day. One day, I believe, I will find my way out or be rescued, and it will all be because of God.

Kevin

The taste of dirt in my mouth is the first thing I notice when I wake up. If you've never experienced it, I don't recommend you try. When I open one eye, I don't know where I am. Two eyes don't improve the view. All I see is dirt, rocks, pine needles but nothing specific that would help me determine my location. A pulsing headache is demanding my attention. I gently raise my hand to my forehead and feel a large lump on it. My situation is dire, but I must think rationally.

I mentally compile a list of all the things I know now. This instantly makes me miss Charlotte and her love of lists again. First, I am lying face down one the ground with a potentially serious head injury and some minor scrapes. Second, I vaguely remember falling yesterday while hiking down the mountain with the Rangers. Third, I am separated from the group and don't have a clue where I am now. Finally, Charlotte and I are both lost now.

I would really like to get up and take stock of my surroundings, and, for the love of Pete, clean this dirt out of my mouth. With my head injured I'm reluctant to sit up. When I lift my head, my stomach threatens to empty its meager contents. Instead, I pull my knees under my torso and use my arms to push up onto all fours. I pause and breathe in nose and out mouth slowly until the wave of pain and dizziness recedes. Moving even a little makes my head swim and my stomach do flips. I stay in this position that Charlotte did in yoga called "tabletop" for several minutes, breathing through the pain until it subsides.

I'm not sure I can stand so I crawl to the nearest tree and sit with my back against it. This small movement leaves me panting and dizzy, but at least now I can see my surroundings instead of just dirt.

When I woke earlier I thought it was morning but that was because I was turned around and couldn't see the sun through the heavy cloud cover. It's getting dark again and I'm disheartened that the only thing I accomplished today was sitting up. The old Chinese proverb that "a journey of a thousand miles begins with a single step" could be modified in my current situation to "begins with sitting up."

I am fatigued and scared and alone. Even in my addled state of mind I know I have to stay alive for Charlotte.

I pray, "Please God, don't like me die like this. Not after everything I've gone through. I know this can't be the end. Help me. Help Charlotte and keep her safe." It's corny, but now I feel safer and more secure even though I'm still alone and defenseless. I've turned the problem over to him.

"I'm coming Charlotte. Hold on," I whisper over and over as I collapse on a bed of pine needles from exhaustion. Tired, hungry, thirsty, and with a mouth full of dirt.

Chapter 26

Day 24

" The best way out is always through."
Unknown

"Let's go!" I shout. I have heard Kev and his friends shout this many times at the TV screen while watching football games. I always found it humorous because the people shouting it had no involvement in the actual "going." But the emotional investment in the game made them feel part of it. Right now it feels right to say it, even though there is no "us", just me. The exclamation makes sense now; I get it.

Today I will paint the last symbol and bring it back to the pool to study the message all together without being limited by time and distance. I mix up hopefully my last batch of paint and take my rock to the cave painting then sit down, feeling hopeful and happy to get this finished today. Anticipation is a beehive buzzing in my belly. The last symbol is a circle with some type of design inside. I paint a large circle first then get up to study the design more closely.

I originally thought it was something more complicated, but it is in fact three zigzag lines stacked on top of each other. Returning to the rock I copy the pattern inside. It takes longer to paint all these lines with my finger. The W above the line could be rays of sun rising above the horizon. Once finished I stare at it dumbfounded. This one has me stumped.

I carry the rock back to the pool and place it at the far left, which would be the final word or phrase of the message. Something clicks inside me, like when you put the last piece in the puzzle. I have some theories about what some of the symbols mean, but together I hope they will make more sense. I grab some lunch and sit down in front of the symbols to think. I've concluded that the first symbol with the line and W means sun or light. It could also refer to morning or even beginning. But I've got my money on sun or light. I'm actually leaning toward "light" because of the line inside of a circle.

The second symbol I have suspected all along had something to do with the moon. I specifically remember from our trip to Egypt that Ra was the sun god and Horus was the moon god. However, there may be another clue though in the symbol: the pupil is filled completely, a solid black circle. Their culture was based on a lunar calendar, and the full moon was considered to have supernatural or religious significance. This belief is still evident in cultures around the world and in books, movies, modern culture and superstition. I'm taking a logical leap that the symbol means full moon.

For the third symbol, I've had some time to think about and I also remember from hieroglyphs that it is an ankh. However, the symbol has a wide range of meanings. It could mean open, eternal life, or peace. This is one of the symbols that will base its meaning from the context. I will have to come back to it.

Feeling frustrated with limited progress I move onto the fourth one. It seems to be more straightforward, thankfully. The vertical rectangle split in two looks like a door. The small line going across could be a bolt or handle. However, the door could be open or shut. This one also is ambiguous and could slow down the discovery and interpretation of the message.

My head is pounding, but I decide to continue on with decoding the message. I wouldn't be able to sleep tonight anyways if I didn't. The last symbol I painted is a circle filled with what looks like zigzag lines. But what could the lines represent? I try to imagine what these ancient people would have been thinking of when they painted it. To modern people it would be a zipper or even the lines on a heart monitor, but neither of these would fit the meaning, obviously. I don't think it is referring to a god or person but to a thing and most of their symbols are about nature. There are three lines which could mean on top of each other or in a sequence or repetition.

Closing my eyes, I try to visualize it. I'm leaning toward them being one after another. What thing in nature is zigzag and occurs in some type of regular sequence? It has to be waves. The circle must represent the boundary or shape of the body of water. The symbol means water, not to drink, but a body of water. I don't think it has to have waves. The lines just distinguish it from an open circle, which would be the sun.

I'm mentally exhausted from all this thinking. I need to let this information percolate while I sleep. I pray as I settle into my bed, "God give me wisdom to discern the message. Guide my thoughts and help me trust you in this as I have learned to trust you in everything else. Be with Kevin and keep him safe."

Kevin

A bird is on top of my head pecking at my hair. What is that? Ouch! I swat at it and it caws loudly in my ear before flying off. There are many unpleasant way to be awakened in the morning: doorbell, dog barking, or a fly landing on your head. I can add being pecked by a bird to the list and make it number one. It's easier waking up today, even though unpleasant, and I can sit up with only mild dizziness. My stomach is cramping and my tongue sticks to the roof of my dry, dirty mouth. I need to sit up, move and look for water. I won't be any good to Charlotte dead from dehydration. I'm guessing it's been at least thirty-six hours without water. This is pushing the limits.

Gripping the tree with both hands, I'm able to slowly stand. My legs are weak and shaky from the fall and dehydration. I definitely won't be running a marathon any time soon. The ground I'm standing on is fairly flat, but I can see the slope of the mountain that I fell and slid down. I can find the general downhill direction by continuing the trajectory of my fall. I know I still have to go down, a very long ways down. The Rangers should already be back to the lodge and I predict I am a day and a half behind them, depending on how long they stopped to search for me.

Thankfully we are down the mountain far enough to have more trees. I start walking downhill, grabbing onto one tree at a time, holding onto each one a moment before taking steps to the next. This is slow going, but I cannot risk falling or further injuries, plus I only have the energy to walk short distances before I need a break.

After walking a while, I sit, leaning back against a tree, completely depleted of energy. I have been going on sheer willpower alone. "Running on fumes," my grandpa would have said. Now my tank is even out of fumes. My muscles are cramping and I know if I don't get some water I won't be going any further, ever. I lean my head back against the trunk of the tree and try to slow down my breathing and heart rate. I rest my eyes for just a moment when a drop of water plops on my forehead. I wake up startled, sit up and look around hoping for more. I stand up, holding onto the tree, and hold my hand out to try to feel raindrops. I don't feel any rain on my arms, but I watch another drop fall in the exact same spot I was just sitting. In fact, that spot looks really damp and now that I think about it, the seat of my pants is damp too. I walk back to the tree and crouch down to look there. It's definitely moist.

Another drop falls and I watch it hit the ground and run in a small rivulet. I couldn't see it under the leaves and pine needles. I bend down and blow them out of the way and follow the crease. The trail of water travels between trees and gets bigger the farther I follow it. After fifty yards of this I start to hear a distant sound that makes me weep with joy: water. The water trail joins a bubbling stream flowing down the mountain.

Raising my head to heaven, I thank God before plunging my whole head into the cold stream. I gargle the water and spit it out, so immensely thankful to get rid of the fuzz and dirt. Then I rinse my hands and cup them, but I only allow myself a few drinks of water. I don't want to get sick. I sit beside the stream and wait for my stomach to settle, taking in this National Geographic worthy view. A frothy white sky is speared by the triangles of mountains. The stream is gurgling and jumping over rocks as if in a NASCAR race to get to the river below. My water-deprived brain has now caught up with the obvious conclusion that the stream would flow into a river below that I can follow. I clap my hands, then cup them around my mouth and yell, "Let's go!" like I do while watching a Steelers' game. With another big drink I hike down the mountain following the stream.

The stream joins a beautiful river that white water rafters would drool after. I've spent most of the day hiking down the slope along the river and have been wet and cold, but at least I'm hydrated. It's not going to be safe for me to hike any more today now that it's getting dark and I'm too tired to look for food. I walk a little away from the river to find a dry bed of pine needles to sleep in tonight.

I pray, "Help me to keep going, God. I can't go on without you. Help Charlotte and keep her safe."

Sleep draws me under. "Don't give up, Charlotte," I whisper into the night.

Chapter 27

Day 25

It's an earthquake! The ground rumbles for a few seconds then stops. The vibration woke me up from a deep sleep. Whatever answers I had figured out yesterday are gone now. The rumbling continues again. This one is more startling than the first because I'm awake now and my brain is functioning enough to be terrified.

Then, after several seconds, it stops again. I place my hand over my chest and my heart feels like it is running in the Kentucky Derby and winning. My breathing is rapid and I am afraid that I'm on the edge of hyperventilating. After just a few seconds, the rumbling vibration starts up again, but this time I count while it is going. One. Two. Three. Four. Five. Six. Seven. Eight. Nine. Ten. Then it stops. The counting actually helped calm me. But all too quickly it starts up again. I tap my leg with a finger counting off the seconds. This one is roughly the same amount of time and when it stops, I count the break in between, only five seconds. The earthquakes continue for what seems like hours although I know it could only be a few minutes.

In my bed I grip the moss and reeds so hard that I can feel them cutting into my palms. It has been going on for a while, and it seems like it is getting louder, but I don't know if that's true or my paranoia. When a couple small rocks break free from a wall on the far side of the cave and roll down, my level of anxiety spikes. I didn't know I could get even more scared. I have a very real fear that this cave could collapse any minute. If this rumbling continues the stalactites could fall.

In my dark moments I had wished and even prayed for one to fall and end my misery. I take it all back. The earthquakes could crack the ceiling and the floor could even fall into whatever is underneath it. The terror of unknown possibilities is paralyzing. I honestly don't know what to do other than just accept my fate.

I have been in this cave now for twenty-five days, and God has protected and provided for me without fail. Why would he bring me this far just to have me crushed inside after this long? During one very dark time in my life, I was in the middle of an anxiety attack, which I now realize was not that bad compared to what I'm going through now, but Reciting Psalm 23 was a big help. I just kept repeating it over and over until I felt the words become true and I felt peace. I don't feel like doing it now, but I also don't feel like being in fear of dying, so I start off quietly and speak through my tears.

"The Lord is my shepherd, I shall not want. He makes me lie down in green pastures, he leads me by still waters, he restores my soul. He leads me in paths of righteousness for his namesake. Yay though I walk through the valley of the shadow of death, I will fear no evil, for you are with me; your rod, and your staff they comfort me. You prepare a table before me in the presence of my enemies, you anoint my head with oil, my cup overflows. Surely goodness and mercy will follow me all the days of my life, and I will dwell in the house of the Lord forever."

I know I didn't get the words perfect, but I think God is ok with that. He's always telling us that it's all about the heart. I repeat the Psalm as the cave rumbles around me. I choke up while praying it. With the rumbling and the crumbling of rocks, it's hard to believe the words. So I start over again, slower, trying to make the words come from my heart and believe that they are true. This time was better, and it brought me an ounce of comfort. I started again and said it louder. There's no fear of loud sounds making rocks fall down because they already are, so I shout the words into the cave. I finished Psalm 23 and I am not exaggerating when I say that the earthquake stopped. Is it possible that the word of God did this? I fall to my knees; my mind is blown away and cannot comprehend that God could do this. I'm humbled by his protection and provision, and I asked him to forgive me for doubting him. I'm trapped in a cave, but I'm loved and provided for by a very big God.

I pray, "God, wherever Kevin is, protect him and keep him safe just like how you're taking care of me."

Kevin

When you wake up dreading the day ahead, you aren't living— you're just surviving the day. I have dreaded waking up every day since Charlotte disappeared. I've been sad and angry and even suicidal at times.

Today is the first day in weeks that I woke up with hope and peace. I know I will find her if I just don't give up. I believe I would feel it if she was dead, but I don't. I search the banks of the river for some edible plants to take the edge off of my hunger and find some cattails that I can eat along the bank.

I'm munching on them and looking around. Downriver leads to the lodge and certain safety. Downriver is also admitting defeat and leaving Charlotte behind permanently. I have determined that I'm not leaving this mountain until I find her, dead or alive.

Eating always makes me think better. Charlotte and I agreed on that. "No good decisions are made on an empty stomach," she would joke Now that I have the river as my guide I can continue to search around more as long as I stay close to it.

But my hopeful reprieve is interrupted by the ground shaking again. I grab onto the nearest tree to keep from being thrown into the river and swept away. The rumbling stops and I let out the breath I didn't know I was holding, but before I can relax the ground shakes again. It lasts just a few seconds like the first one. Then the ground shakes again and this time rocks the size of basketballs and small cars break loose and roll down the mountain. I take cover behind the biggest tree around. This earthquake is bigger and longer and when it ends I walk around taking in the destruction caused in such a short period of time. I see a rock slide higher up the mountain and small cracks in the ground and bedrock. I've studied sites around the world that were destroyed by major earthquakes. Where there is one earthquake, there will be more.

This mountain and valley must be on a fault line. Seismic and even tectonic movement under the surface of the mountain could have created a crack or hole down into a cave inside mountain. From geology I learned that rocks will break in predictable patterns along their lines of cleavage. When there's an earthquake the rock will break and later on re-break, many times forming caves, especially between layers of different rocks. The earthquake seemed to be focused on the upper part of the mountain.

We haven't had many clues to go on during our search. This earthquake has led me to believe that it is possible that Charlotte could be trapped somewhere in this mountain.

I pray, "God, this time I'm dead serious. Keep Charlotte safe. Send angels to protect her. Let my love for her guide my feet back to her heart."

Chapter 28

Day 26

My dreams were riddled with boulders chasing me and stalactites impaling me. My body wakes up rested, but my mind is exhausted from the parade of bad dreams marching through my subconscious all night like a bad high school marching band. I'm scared to get out of bed but even more scared to stay here.

My bladder and stomach win the debate and I head to the pool. After I'm sated I sit beside the pool with my face in my hands. And I cry. I've been positive for several days, but this is an aftershock cry. I'm crying because I was so terrified that I was going to die and never see Kevin again. I'm crying tears of joy and happiness to still be alive. My head pounds from the roller-coaster of emotion and bad sleep.

I feel the need to wash off the dust from the rumbling of the earthquake, so I strip down and wade into the pool. It is warm and refreshing and so calming, as always. I rinse my hair and feel my headache rinse away like shampoo. While floating on my back I feel completely supported, cared for, and carefree. It's like that verse, "Cast your cares upon the Lord for he cares for you." I enjoy this moment, really absorb the break from worry and fear.

The pool is a kaleidoscope of colors. The waterfall from the stream creates a soft spray of diamonds on the black satin of the cave. The edges of the pool are emerald green blending down into midnight blue then the deepest part of the pool is inky black.

This pool has magic powers, but I've been suspicious and haven't fully trusted it. I've been scared to do more than tread water, float and swim underwater briefly. I can only touch bottom about six feet into the pool; it seems to have very steep sides. I've been treading water in the near center, but I'm curious to explore underneath me. Before I can chicken-out I take in a deep breath and dive down. It gets dark quickly and I can't see past my hands. I kick my feet hard and swim down farther. I started counting when I dove down and it's been twenty-seconds until I touch something solid with my hands. I feel around a little bit, but it seems to be all sand. I keep exploring until I have to come up for air.

I break the surface and catch my breath. I assume that would have been the deepest part of the pool so next dive I go down about halfway to the shore. When

I swim down and touch bottom it is sand that has rock underneath, sloping steeply down to the middle. I test this at various spot around the pool and all have sand at the bottom. I'm breathing heavy after four dives so I float in the middle to catch my breath and think. The pool seems to be shaped like a funnel. I need to check the center again. With an extra big breath I dive down in the center and feel around the sand, trying to clear it away to figure out what, if anything, is underneath. What I notice is that there are large flat rocks with cracks in between, almost like a seam or fine grout lines. It feels like there is current flowing down through the cracks. Running out of time and air, I rise to the surface with a theory about the pool.

I don't know why I haven't noticed this in over three weeks, but there aren't any streams leading out from the pool. The only other place water could exit would be within the pool. That means there is a way out of the cave, albeit a small one. I thought the cracks in the walls could be my exit, but I may have been looking for the wrong cracks.

My diving has used up most of the day. I sit by the pool today and eat, processing everything I learned today. The diving burned a lot of calories, and I have to eat more to refuel. The way out of the cave is opened every twenty-eight days, so I know the when and today I think I might know where. Now I have to work out how.

Before bed I pray, "Thank you for your miraculous provision. I shouldn't be alive now for several reasons, but you have kept protected and sustained me. God, help me find the way out. Open my eyes to the truth. I trust you. Please, please, please keep Kevin safe."

Kevin

Hiking along a river that flows down a steep mountain valley is hazardous and time-consuming. The park had made a nice, smooth gravel trail for the hike. This is not a hike; it is climbing over boulders and wading through swampy mud for hours only to have covered a mile at most. I'm being as careful as I can in my circumstances, but I feel confident about my direction by staying close to the river. Plus, I have some food and all the water I can drink.

Taking regular breaks can help prevent injury because I'm not at full strength yet. After a full day of hiking I wrap up the day by sitting on top of a large boulder, looking up at the mountain that I know Charlotte is trapped in. It's been cloudy and drizzling all day, just enough to make you want a nap, but this evening the sky has cleared and I see the pink of the sunset peeking behind the mountain. It truly is a beautiful sight, but I would like it a lot more if my wife wasn't inside it. I wish we could be enjoying this view together. A wave of grief crashes over me, threatening to take me under.

"She's gone because you're a failure," a voice whispers. "You can't even climb down a mountain without getting hurt, how do you expect to rescue her? The world would be better without you in it. Nobody would miss you."

These negative messages settle into my brain like fog on a humid night. It would be so easy to believe them and just lie down beside this river and give up. However, these are not my thoughts!

Those tempting lies try to suck me under like a riptide. If I do nothing I will die in their seductive, destructive waves. I recognize them for what they are: lies from the enemy. I've come too far to accept them. I'm not going to listen to them anymore; they have to go. Spiritual warfare is as simple as speaking the name of Jesus, declaring the word of God.

"Get out of my head devil!" I shout since no one is around to hear me. "You're not welcome here any more because I have the mind of Christ!" I kneel beside the river in the cold mud and pray, "Help me, Jesus. I can't do this without you." I recite Psalm ninety-one quietly until I feel the oppression leave my mind. God's peace settles on me like grandma's quilt.

The mountain looks slightly different since the last time I saw it clearly. The earthquake probably caused the snow to slide down or maybe even an avalanche. I wouldn't know miles away from it down here. I rub my eyes because what I'm seeing can't be what I'm seeing. Nope. Still there. There is a waterfall cascading down the side of the mountain that was definitely not there yesterday. It looks like it flows down into a pool which is the headwaters of the river. The last rays of the sun glint off the waterfall, making it look like crystal. It is so beautiful. I weep at how God can take something so destructive and create beauty from it. This was a sign.

"Give me strength, Lord. I know I'm close. Bring us back together," I pray then fall asleep on the riverbank.

Chapter 29

Day 27

"If you can't fly then run, if you can't run then walk, if you can't walk then crawl, but whatever you do you have to keep moving forward."
Martin Luther King Jr.

Even though I wake up after another full night of sleep, my brain already feels like it pulled an "all-nighter" before finals. My mind whirled all night like a jacked-up hamster on a wheel. I know the answer is there somewhere between all the clues. Just like a camera, I need to bring the answer into focus.

Here's what I know. First, there are cracks in the wall on the far side of the cave that occasionally have air flowing through them. The cave is either on the side of a mountain or connected to tunnels in the mountain that have fresh air flowing though them. Second, there are more cracks in the bottom of the pool. The water is slowly draining down through the sand and between the large rocks. Water always flows downhill and joins up with other water, following the path of least resistance. Where there's a little water, there will be more if you follow it. Finally, ancient people left a painting behind with a message in it, I believe, showing how to escape in a twenty-eight day cycle. I need to finish translating and interpreting it because day twenty-seven is almost up, and I'm not certain what to expect tomorrow. Suddenly it feels like twenty-eight days have gone in a flash.

Today's task is to finally decode the message from the painting. The symbols all have ancient Egyptian symbols, or some version of them. This mountain is a long way from Egypt, but there could be many scenarios for why these people were writing with those symbols. I have identified the symbols independently but have yet to be able to combine them into a cohesive thought. Modern people today would not use only five words to express something this complex and specific. We describe with adjectives and adverbs and figurative language. However, ancient people didn't use prepositions and articles like we do. The reader had to fill in the blanks between each character. Thus, I need to "read between the lines."

The five symbols are light (or sun), full moon, open, door, pool. In that order. I try inserting various prepositions and articles to see if any of them make those words a cohesive thought, like a sentence. Light (in the) full moon open (a) door (beside the) pool. It could also be: Light (of the) full moon open(s) the door (inside) pool.

Honestly, any of these could be correct so I will have to research each one to determine what the correct interpretation is. Where is the door? That is really the only unknown. I think of all the directions a door could be in relation to the pool: above, below, beside (left or right), and in front of. A door has to have seams, which could be cracks of some sort, and not necessarily in straight lines. I examine the areas around the pool with this in mind. Of course there are cracks everywhere, but none seem to connect to make an opening that could be used by a human. I pace around the pool, frustrated with my lack of success. I thought I had a breakthrough. After a break and a snack, I conclude that the only cracks I didn't examine were the ones in the pool.

It makes sense. The shape of the pool, how it flattens out at the bottom, and the drainage of water through the cracks. The message is "The light of the full moon opens the door inside the pool." I'm not sure how the door opens, but I feel confident that something is going to happen in the pool tomorrow.

Anticipation bubbles in my belly like the aerator in a fish tank. So many "what if's" are floating around in he air. "What if I'm wrong? What if I miss it? What if I never get out? What if Kevin dies while searching for me What if I'm going crazy and I don't even know it?" These doubts are swarming my head, looking for a weak spot to attack. I sit beside the pool and cover my head with my hands, like it could actually keep the thoughts out. A small rational voice is my brain is telling me the thoughts are an attack. I don't have to let them in my head. I stand up, raise my hands and speak the name of Jesus.

"Jesus!" I yell into the cave. "Jesus!" I shout at the thoughts. I close my eyes and pray, "Jesus, you said you would never leave me. Show me you are with me now."

The attack of doubts on my mind has ceased. The normal quiet of the cave is quieter, but the light is brighter. The pool has been behind me while I prayed so I didn't see God's answer. A beam of light is shining straight on the pool and is being refracted into millions of diamonds around the cave. It's like a diamond disco ball lighting up the pool. My mouth is wide open in wonder. This is my answer; he is here right now.

The light is dancing around the cave in an unknown rhythm, turning the drab grays and browns of the rocks into multi-colored minerals. When the lights shine on the cave mural I gasp in shock; it glows. The paintings I made from the gypsum powder are iridescent, too. The handprints that surround the mural all shimmer and I have a sudden desire to add mine to them. It feels sacrilegious, but it would be wrong if I didn't leave something of me behind. There's not much light left today so I move quickly to get my mixing bowl and scrape gypsum powder. The hands on the wall are all lefties, but I really want to do both of mine as a way of distinguishing myself. Adding water, I coat the palm of both hands and walk over to the cave mural. My hands are shaking; I am joining my hands with those across centuries.

I count to ten while pressing my hands firmly to the wall. There are tears running down my cheeks. I'm crying because of the heaviness of this moment but also because I'm scared. I think, "If they could escape, then I can too."

I wash my hands back at the pool and pray, "God, help me be ready for when you move. I sense it coming. Help me trust you that no matter what happens, I will have peace in following you because you are good. Help Kevin. I don't know what he needs, but you do. God, may tomorrow be the day I get to see him again."

I determine to get a good night's sleep and wake early. I will be spending the day beside the pool tomorrow, waiting on God to make something happen.

Kevin

It's been twenty-seven days since I've seen Charlotte. I'm so tired. Like in my bones. I wake up and drink river water and eat crappy grass that barely keeps the hunger at bay. Then I hike. I just pray with each step that I am one step closer to her. That's all that's kept me going. I will either find her or die trying because I don't have the strength or energy to turn around.

"God, I'm putting all my eggs in Your basket that she's still here and alive," I pray. And keep hiking.

After mid-day my strength gives out. My cargo pants are torn, my jacket has been ripped to shreds, and I haven't shaved in a month. The list goes on: my feet have bloody sores, face and lips sunburned and windburned, palms cut up, but worst of all, I smell. I must look like a homeless mountain man. I get a drink of water from the river and with shaking arms and legs sit back against a tree. I dream so much of thick burgers and salty french fries with malted milk shakes until my mouth waters. I fantasize about snuggling with Charlotte on the coach in front of the fireplaces a soft mattress. These daydreams are my mountain mirages. When you desire something so badly that your brain makes you think it is real. This is my rock bottom. The thought of going back has tempted me many times; I have nothing to go back to. I'm going to stay here until God says go.

With cracked lips I only have the strength for one word, "Jesus."

Chapter 30

Day 28

"I am stronger than I am broken."
Roxanne Gay

I really did mean to wake up early. Instead, a bubbling noise wakes me up with a start, like the sound of hot tub jets being turned on. I sit up, stretch and rub my eyes. What is that sound? I can count all the sounds in this cave on one hand and this is not one. I wonder, I'm in a rock cave, what could be making that noise? As soon as I stand up I see the source of the sound. The normally calm pool is swirling and bubbling like letting the water out of a bathtub.

You may not believe that God directs our lives and I didn't truly until my stint here. David said in Psalms, "Before I was born all my days were written in your book before there was yet one." I know that I have made bad and selfish choices, but God has been guiding, directing, and nudging me by his Spirit to live the wonderful life full of blessing that he has prepared for me. Whatever happens today, God is in control, and I trust that he will work it out for my good. Not sure how he's going to pull this one off, but God's hobby is doing the unexpected.

I feel drawn to the pool as if a super magnet was pulling me. I stand on the edge and watch the bubbles rise up from the depths. The water is slowly draining like a bathtub. I feel compelled to get in the pool.

The message said, "The light of the full moon opens the door inside the pool." Jumping in is illogical and extremely dangerous, but I have to take a literal leap of faith. This pool has healed me over and over so I can't believe it would kill me now. I count, one, two, three and jump.

Unlike other times I've been in, there is a strong current. The funnel shape of the pool pulls me down quickly, swirling me towards the center. I sink down feet first and pray for God's protection. The farther I sink the more suction I feel until I feel rock under me. My feet find an opening in the rock and I wiggle into it then get sucked into a tunnel. It was like going through the tube of a waterslide at an amusement park. I can't see where I'm going, but the current is directing me. I want to scream, but I know if I do I will swallow water . I lean back, cross my arms over my chest like a mummy and make myself as small as possible.

The tunnel winds down in a serpentine pattern much like you would expect. Each foot away from the pool the tunnel gets lighter and wider, and I am terrified of what is ahead. Now I can hold my head above water in the tunnel and suck in mouthfuls of fresh air. I can hear a roaring sound getting closer and don't have time to prepare for another challenge, but is inevitable. The tunnel shoots me out over the edge of a waterfall into a lake. I'm bobbing up and down in the cold lake and trying to tread water to get farther away from the crash and current of the waterfall. I look around the lake as I tread water. After so long in the cave I have completely lost my sense of direction. As I swim away from the waterfall, the current is gently flowing to the right and I head that direction. A beautiful river begins its journey here. There is a small log floating a few feet away and I swim toward it, hooking my arms over it.

The cave has been my home for so long and now the great outdoors feel ominous. I feel more alone out here, alone, exposed, lost and floating on this lazy river, than I ever did in the cave. My future is unknown and un-predictable and I am unprepared to face anything that happens from here on out. I wasn't able to think about what would happen after I escaped the cave.

At this moment while floating on a log down a river, I reflect on what I just went through. I fell through a crack into a cave and didn't die. I had water and food provided for me. I escaped the cave into a river that hopefully leads eventually to a town where I can get help. It could have been worse, much worse. At any moment of any day I could have died from a hundred different things.

This reflection turns my mood from woe to wow. I have sunlight; it's so bright that it hurts my eyes. I have fresh air; I can smell the river and pines. A smile begins to sprout on my face. My cheeks hurt because I haven't smiled in so long. I tilt my head back to see the blue sky and puffy clouds. The old hymn comes back to me and I start singing it. "When peace like a river attendeth my way. When sorrows like sea billows roll. Whatever my lot thou hast taught me to say, 'It is well, it is well with my soul!'" I sing it first quietly, almost reverently, but the words fit my life perfectly so I sing it again louder, not caring if I'm off-key. And I believe it, no matter what happens, it is well with my soul. God will take care of me.

I float so long and peacefully on the river that I drift off to sleep sporadically. I wake with jerk when my log gets stuck on the sandy and rocky shallows of the bank of the river. My fingers are pruny from being in the water so long and sitting on a warm rock in the sun sounds heavenly. I pull the log up the bank a little farther to keep it from floating away. Right now it's my only hope for further transportation. A large smooth boulder sits up high above the river so I climb up and look around. I can see the river winding down through the forrest with no visible signs of houses or towns. This discourages me, but I remember that it took Kevin and I two days to hike up the mountain. I don't know how long I've floated down the river, but I'm guessing I have a long ways left.

The sun is getting lower in the sky and I know it will be dark in this canyon sooner here than other places. Thank God it's warm. My clothes have dried a little while sitting on the rock and the sand is still warm. I dig out a shallow pit in the sand to lay down it. The sand is the softest thing I've slept on in a month. It all feels surreal, but I doze peacefully.

Heavy footsteps wake me up with a start. I'm scared to attract attention and get eaten by a bear, so I make myself as small as possible in my hole. I can't tell if this sound is from an animal or human. The crunching gets closer and I must make a sound because the person walks toward the sound.

"Who's there?" a male voice asks quietly. I remain quiet. "Whoever you are, I won't hurt you." He is looking my direction but above me.

I raise my head an inch to see the man. He's tall and stocky in a tattered plaid shirt with the sleeves rolled up to his elbows. He has on ripped cargo pants and a torn jacket tied around his waist. He looks dangerous. A full beard obscures his sunburned face but he has laugh lines around his eyes. I gasp and he hears me. It can't be.

"It can't be," his words echo my thoughts. He runs over and kneels down in front of me. It's him, Kevin. He's here beside this unknown river in the mountains.

"Kevin! Kevin! It's really you Kevin!" I jump up out of my sand hole and wrap my arms around his neck, knocking him back onto the sand. "Am I dreaming?"

"This should answer your question." Then he kisses me, crushing me to him, like he won't get to ever again. It is sweet and passionate. My salty tears make this less than idyllic, but he doesn't seem to mind. We pull apart and just stare at each other. He strokes my cheek tenderly. "If this is a dream don't wake me up."

"What are you doing here?" I ask, looking for the answer in his blue eyes. "I mean, I'm ridiculously happy that you're here, but why? How?"

Kevin kisses my ear and whispers, "I'm here for you, Char. I've never given up looking for you. I knew you didn't die or run away. I just knew." He brushes a strand of hair behind my ear. "Just like I knew God would take care of you."

"I've been alone for so long that mind was beginning to play tricks on me. Was everything before the cave just a dream? I believed God would take care of me and rescue me, but it was really hard sometimes, actually all the time. But even when I doubted, God never stopped. He is the reason I'm alive. He's not done with me, or you, or us." I kiss him again. Our kiss communicates more than my words can right now. This intimacy is intoxicating after so many years of being busy and distracted and a month of being separated. It feels brand new. God has protected me, healed me, rescued me and now restored me and our marriage. Now it's time to go home. Home isn't a house— it's the location of our hearts.

Kevin

The ground is vibrating again and wakes me up. Not violently like the earthquake but like the gurgles and rumbles you get in your stomach when it's upset or hungry. I can stand and walk slowly with my knees bent to keep my balance, but something is going on under the surface. There is a sense of anticipation in the air like how you can smell rain right before it starts and the birds get quiet. I look up at the mountain.

"God, let today be the day," I pray. I get a drink of water and begin my zombie march upriver. The river has started to climb in elevation more, so it takes more energy to cover less distance than yesterday. In my weakened state I have to take frequent breaks.

I'm resting against a tree, dozing off and on, when the rumbling has stopped and restarted again. Then I hear a loud whoosh, like the sound of the world's largest toilet flushing. I follow the noise and see a burst of water shoot out of the opening where the waterfall comes out. A mixture of rocks fly out with the water, landing in the pool below the waterfall. Then all is silent except for the soft spray of the waterfall back to its normal flow. I lean my head back and rest again. My physical stamina is no longer able to keep up with my mental will power.

A roar is building from the level of a fly buzzing to The river is sound volume is increasing from the water level rising, and it interrupts my nap. The water level is higher and rushing violently down the mountain. There is more debris in it than before, and I scan the water for anything useful.

Just upriver ten feet from where I am resting is a sandy alcove. It's strewn with sticks and small logs from the river. It looks like a small animal is burrowed down in the sound. I worry that it could be a dangerous or wounded, but it would've attacked me while I was napping if it thought I was a threat. As I walk closer it's obvious that it is a person, and my heart rate spikes, both in anticipation and fear.

I ask, "Who's there? Whoever you are, I won't hurt you." The person's head raises out of the sand. "It can't be," I whisper. I've been searching all this time and now that I've found her I can't believe it. It felt like I was going to search for her the rest of my life, and I would have if needed.

She jumps up out of the sand and wraps her arms around my neck, knocking me down with a grunt. "Am I dreaming?" she asks me, staring down at me with hazel eyes and her hair in wild braids.

"This should answer your question," I reply and kiss her breathless. "If I'm dreaming don't wake me up."

Every dollar, every second, every hurt, all of it, was worth it. My head is spinning and heart is full. I don't know how we're going to get off this mountain, but I know we'll do it together. God has rescued us, and the joy now is greater than all the sorrow combined.

"Charlotte, my wild Cavewoman, you are the queen of my heart. Are you ready to go home?"

She holds both of my hands in her small ones, intertwining them. "Anywhere with you is home."

Chapter 31

Epilogue

Charlotte and Kevin

It's a typical rainy Saturday morning in Pittsburgh during late fall. We have been back in the States a few weeks. Moses, our chocolate lab, naps on the rug in front of the fireplace. Kevin and I are snuggled on the couch under his grandma's quilt, still in our pajamas even though it's almost noon. We're sipping steamy cups of herbal tea. I haven't been able to drink coffee since the cave. It's crazy that I'm unemployed, and that doesn't bother me one bit. A month in a cave will chill you out.

It took us a week to get home with all the mess of getting off the mountain and getting back into the States. Sita and Pelo nursed us back to health. My father had to pull more strings to get us home because some people were suspicious about our activities. When we tell people our story, we get the response, "Oh really. Wow. That's...incredible." It's very possible we are being monitored by Homeland Security. We don't blame them; we have no proof: no pictures or evidence of anything. If it hadn't happened to us, we probably wouldn't believe it either.

We are thankful for the selfless people who helped us: Pelo and Sita and the Rangers. Charlotte's father demonstrated his love in a way that he has never been able to verbalize to her. Her mother unexpectedly took care of all the little things that needed done back home. God even answers unasked prayers. But watch out for those prayers where you tell God that you'll do anything; he'll take you up on that.

Later today we are having lunch with Charlotte's parents. It's a miracle just to get them in the same room. Who knows? Maybe God has more than one marriage in mind to restore.

Charlotte went to work when we got home to quit her job, but they beat her to it by firing her after being gone three days without calling in, which is hilarious. Kevin is still on sabbatical from work and we are...reevaluating what's important in our lives. Whatever we do, it will be an "us" thing.

Our priorities have been completely redefined. God first, our marriage second, then our careers last. Hopefully we can add children to that list in the near future. Our old church that we went to twice a year was replaced by a nondenominational one with modern worship and small groups for discipleship. We started counseling to work on our issues and deal with the trauma from the experience. Having a bad relationship takes no effort, but it's hard work to have a healthy one.

We have prayed and put it all in God's hands: our marriage, relationships, finances, and careers. We trust that we will feel his nudging when it's time to take the next step. No matter what, God will take care of us. That's what God taught this Cavewoman and her Mountain Man.

About the Author

If you googled my name you have already discovered that J.N. Foxe is a pen name. If I wrote with my actual name and you googled me, you might not have bought this book. Christians are good at forgiving certain sins, but there's other that are just too bad, even though in God's eyes all are sins are equal. In real life I have several labels slapped on me much like Hester in <u>The Scarlet Letter</u> or Rahab in the Bible. I have tried to reinvent myself beyond them and have found that one way to do so is behind the safety of my keyboard...to give the world a story that illustrates the struggles of mental health and the continual road of stability and recovery from everything life throws at us. My intent was to help misfits like me cope with these hurdles of addiction, anger, depression, mania, anxiety, control issues, co-dependency, etc. One day in a future book this paragraph might reveal more, but today this is all I can do and I'm ok with that. "One day at a time" has been my mantra and saving grace for years of my ongoing recovery. And it's true. Find a way out of whatever cave you're trapped in with God's help. Face the world after you get out. I'm working on it and ask you to continue this journey with me.

With all my love and prayers,

J.N. Foxe

Credits

- Because I know you're finished with the story it doesn't matter how much or little I write here. (Does anyone even read these anyways?) There are no grammatical rules for a credits page, so I decided to do bullet points. Since I'm self-publishing I can do what I want. Please do not argue over the order as there is no order.
- My husband, I sat here for several minutes crying because I literally can't find the words. I don't deserve you. The world would be a better place with more men like you.
- My beautiful daughter, you were the one who said, "Mom, you can still write that book."
- Celebrate Recovery, the first place I took off the mask— all of the masks and found out I wasn't alone.
- Candice, it's a beautiful thing to open up and not be judged. How many times in open share did we yell, "Me too!" Thank you for your input and editing services, friend.
- Mom and Dad - without your help and support through rough years this never would've happened.

· Bubba, believe it or not you inspired a few characters. You are always the first person to help.

· Meine schwester, it blessed my heart when after you read a few chapters you wanted to share it with people who were hurting. I wanted you to wait till it was finished...so share away!

· Rock - you wrote and published a book, so I thought if HE can do it then I can too!

Author Bio

J.N. Foxe is a first-time author with a mild addiction to hot tea and reading on her Kindle. She loves to craft, cook, and walk along the Ohio River with her mastiff, Winchester. She is married to a loving husband with the patience of a tortoise. They have two amazing (nearly) grown kids that prove God's grace is real—they're awesome in spite of many failures. Music has always been central in life; she currently plays and sings in her church's praise band. This book took a year-and-a-half to write because Charlotte and the author were both trying to get out of that cave. What will they do now?